GEORGE O'CONNOR

APHRODITE
GODDESS OF LOVE

A NEAL PORTER BOOK

First Second
New York

IN THE TIME BEFORE TIME,
THERE WAS NOTHING, KAOS.

FROM OUT OF KAOS CAME GE,
OR GAEA, OUR MOTHER EARTH.

BUT SHE WAS NOT ALONE.

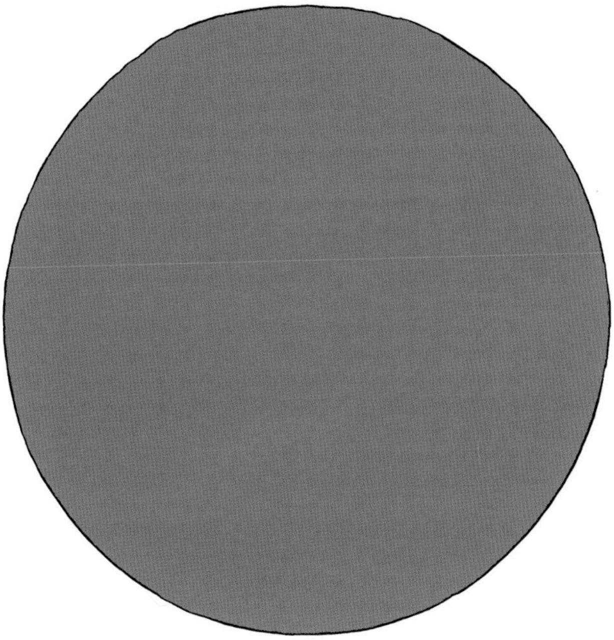

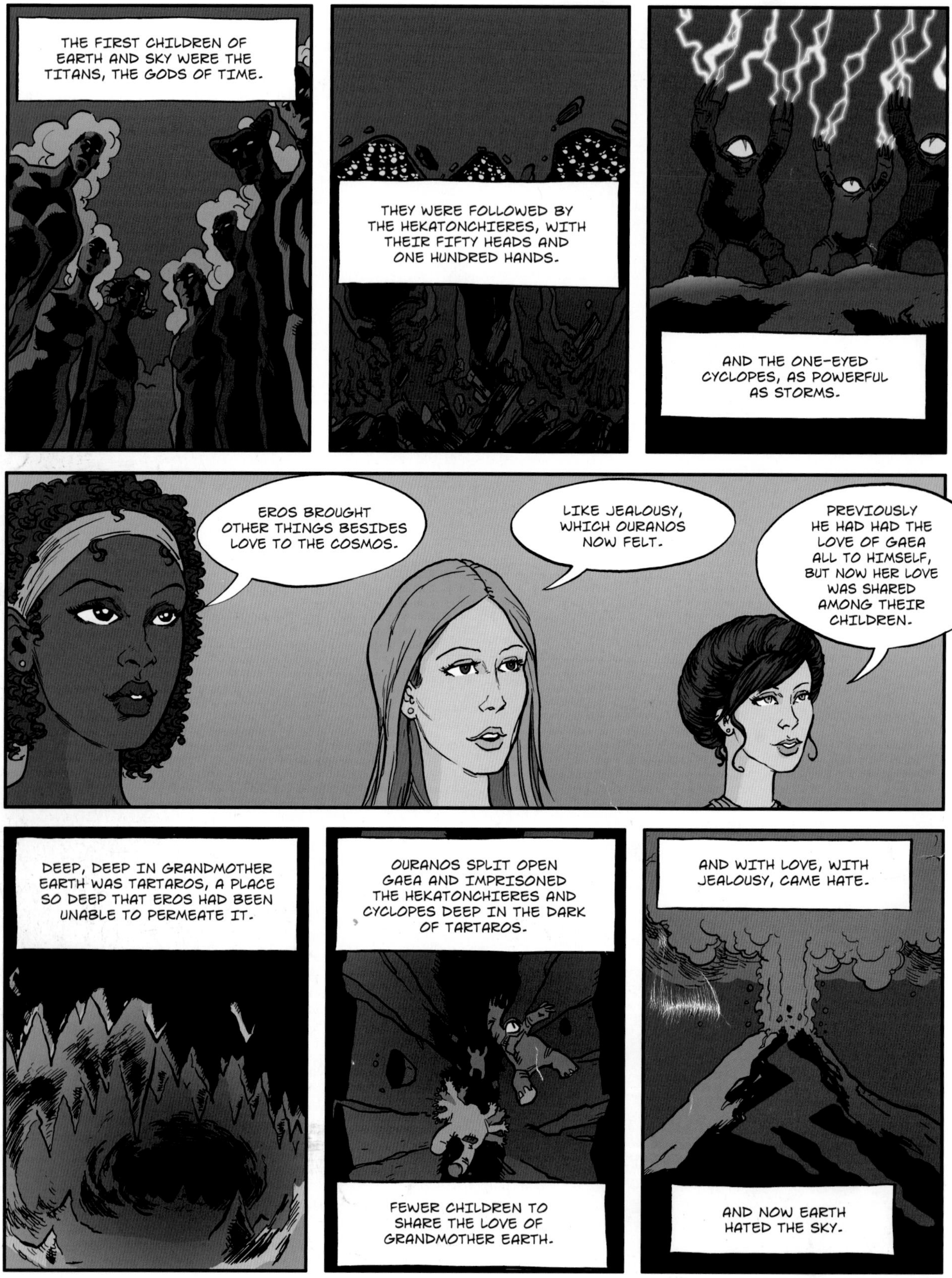
THE FIRST CHILDREN OF EARTH AND SKY WERE THE TITANS, THE GODS OF TIME.
THEY WERE FOLLOWED BY THE HEKATONCHIERES, WITH THEIR FIFTY HEADS AND ONE HUNDRED HANDS.
AND THE ONE-EYED CYCLOPES, AS POWERFUL AS STORMS.
EROS BROUGHT OTHER THINGS BESIDES LOVE TO THE COSMOS.
LIKE JEALOUSY, WHICH OURANOS NOW FELT.
PREVIOUSLY HE HAD HAD THE LOVE OF GAEA ALL TO HIMSELF, BUT NOW HER LOVE WAS SHARED AMONG THEIR CHILDREN.
DEEP, DEEP IN GRANDMOTHER EARTH WAS TARTAROS, A PLACE SO DEEP THAT EROS HAD BEEN UNABLE TO PERMEATE IT.
OURANOS SPLIT OPEN GAEA AND IMPRISONED THE HEKATONCHIERES AND CYCLOPES DEEP IN THE DARK OF TARTAROS.
FEWER CHILDREN TO SHARE THE LOVE OF GRANDMOTHER EARTH.
AND WITH LOVE, WITH JEALOUSY, CAME HATE.
AND NOW EARTH HATED THE SKY.

THE SEAT OF EROS'S POWER IN OURANOS FELL TO THE EARTH.

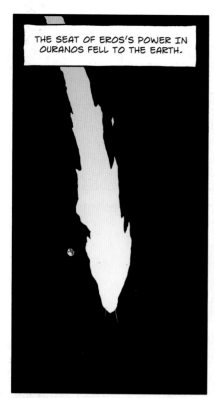

IT WAS SWALLOWED BY THE SEAS THAT GIRD MOTHER EARTH.

THE FOAM THAT TRAILED FROM THE SEVERED PIECE OF SKY CHURNED AND ROILED FOR AN AGE.

POWERLESS, IMPOTENT, OURANOS FLED TO THE FAR REACHES OF THE COSMOS.

IMPOSSIBLY DISTANT, BUT STILL VISIBLE.

THE SCARS OF A LOVE DESTROYED.

UNDER THE SWAY OF EROS, THE TITANS CAME TOGETHER, AND BROUGHT FORTH NEW GENERATIONS.

ONLY THE HEKATONCHIERES AND THE CYCLOPES, IMPRISONED STILL IN TARTAROS, WERE IMMUNE TO ITS TOUCH.

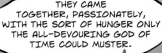

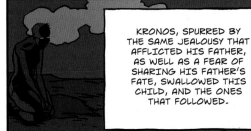

KRONOS THE USURPER AND HIS QUEEN, RHEA, FELT THE PULL OF EROS.

THEY CAME TOGETHER, PASSIONATELY, WITH THE SORT OF HUNGER ONLY THE ALL-DEVOURING GOD OF TIME COULD MUSTER.

THE OFFSPRING THAT RESULTED FROM THIS UNION WERE UNLIKE ANYTHING THE WORLD HAD SEEN BEFORE.

KRONOS, SPURRED BY THE SAME JEALOUSY THAT AFFLICTED HIS FATHER, AS WELL AS A FEAR OF SHARING HIS FATHER'S FATE, SWALLOWED THIS CHILD, AND THE ONES THAT FOLLOWED.

BUT GRANDMOTHER EARTH DECEIVED KRONOS AND HID ONE CHILD AWAY. THAT CHILD, ZEUS, GREW UP TO FREE HIS SIBLINGS AND OVERTHROW KRONOS.

AND STILL THE WATERS FROTHED AND SEETHED.

ZEUS AND THESE NEW GODS, THE OLYMPIANS, WERE NO STRANGERS TO EROS'S POWER.

THEY COUPLED WITH ONE ANOTHER, WITH OTHER BEINGS, WITH MONSTERS, EVEN WITH HUMANS.

AND IN TURN, THEY PRODUCED MORE GODS, MORE HEROES, MORE MONSTERS...

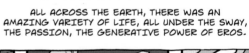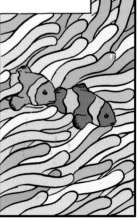

ALL ACROSS THE EARTH, THERE WAS AN AMAZING VARIETY OF LIFE, ALL UNDER THE SWAY, THE PASSION, THE GENERATIVE POWER OF EROS.

STILL WITHOUT A FOCUS, OR A CENTER, OR A GUIDING INTELLIGENCE. BUT EVERYWHERE, AND WITHIN EVERYONE.

THEN, ONE DAY, THE SWIRLING FROTH THAT SEETHED AND SIMMERED FROM THE SEVERED PORTION OF OURANOS, THE PORTION THAT HAD HOUSED HIS OWN EROS—

—CREATED A MIND FOR ITSELF.

AND, SUDDENLY, EROS WAS AWARE.

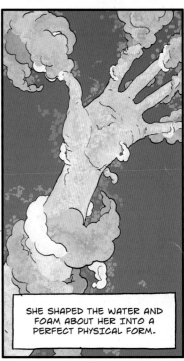

SHE SHAPED THE WATER AND FOAM ABOUT HER INTO A PERFECT PHYSICAL FORM.

DO YOU REMEMBER THAT DAY, SISTERS? I DOUBT ANY WHO LIVED THEN COULD EVER FORGET, WOULD EVER *WANT* TO FORGET.

THE POWER OF EROS,
GIVEN FLESH AT LAST.

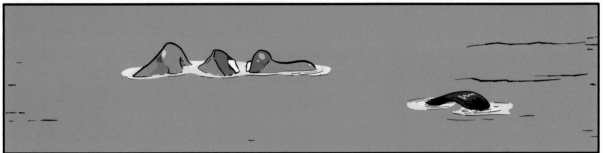

SHE HEADED TOWARD THE
SHORE OF THE NEAREST
ISLAND, CALLED CYPRUS.

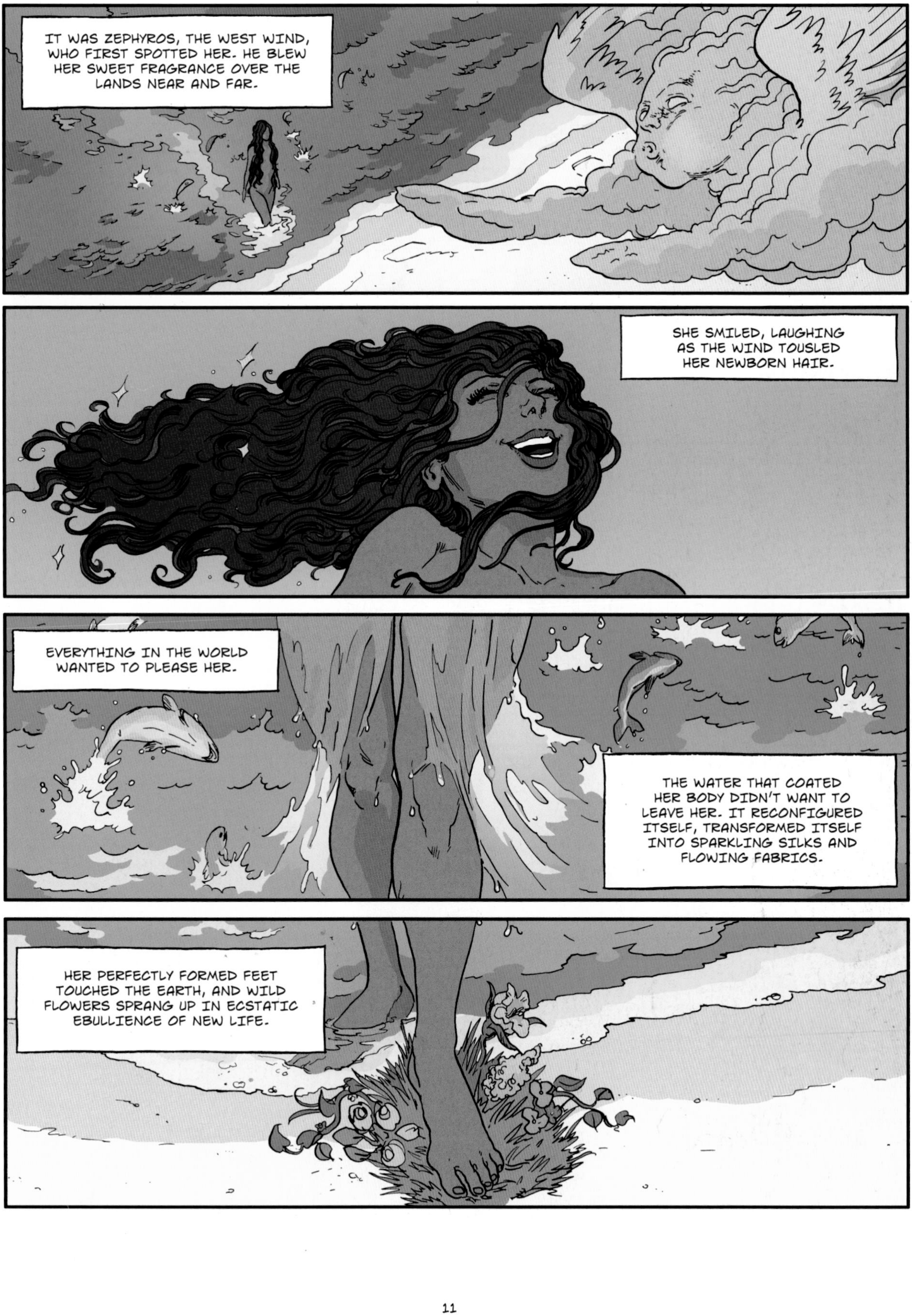
IT WAS ZEPHYROS, THE WEST WIND, WHO FIRST SPOTTED HER. HE BLEW HER SWEET FRAGRANCE OVER THE LANDS NEAR AND FAR.
SHE SMILED, LAUGHING AS THE WIND TOUSLED HER NEWBORN HAIR.
EVERYTHING IN THE WORLD WANTED TO PLEASE HER.
THE WATER THAT COATED HER BODY DIDN'T WANT TO LEAVE HER. IT RECONFIGURED ITSELF, TRANSFORMED ITSELF INTO SPARKLING SILKS AND FLOWING FABRICS.
HER PERFECTLY FORMED FEET TOUCHED THE EARTH, AND WILD FLOWERS SPRANG UP IN ECSTATIC EBULLIENCE OF NEW LIFE.

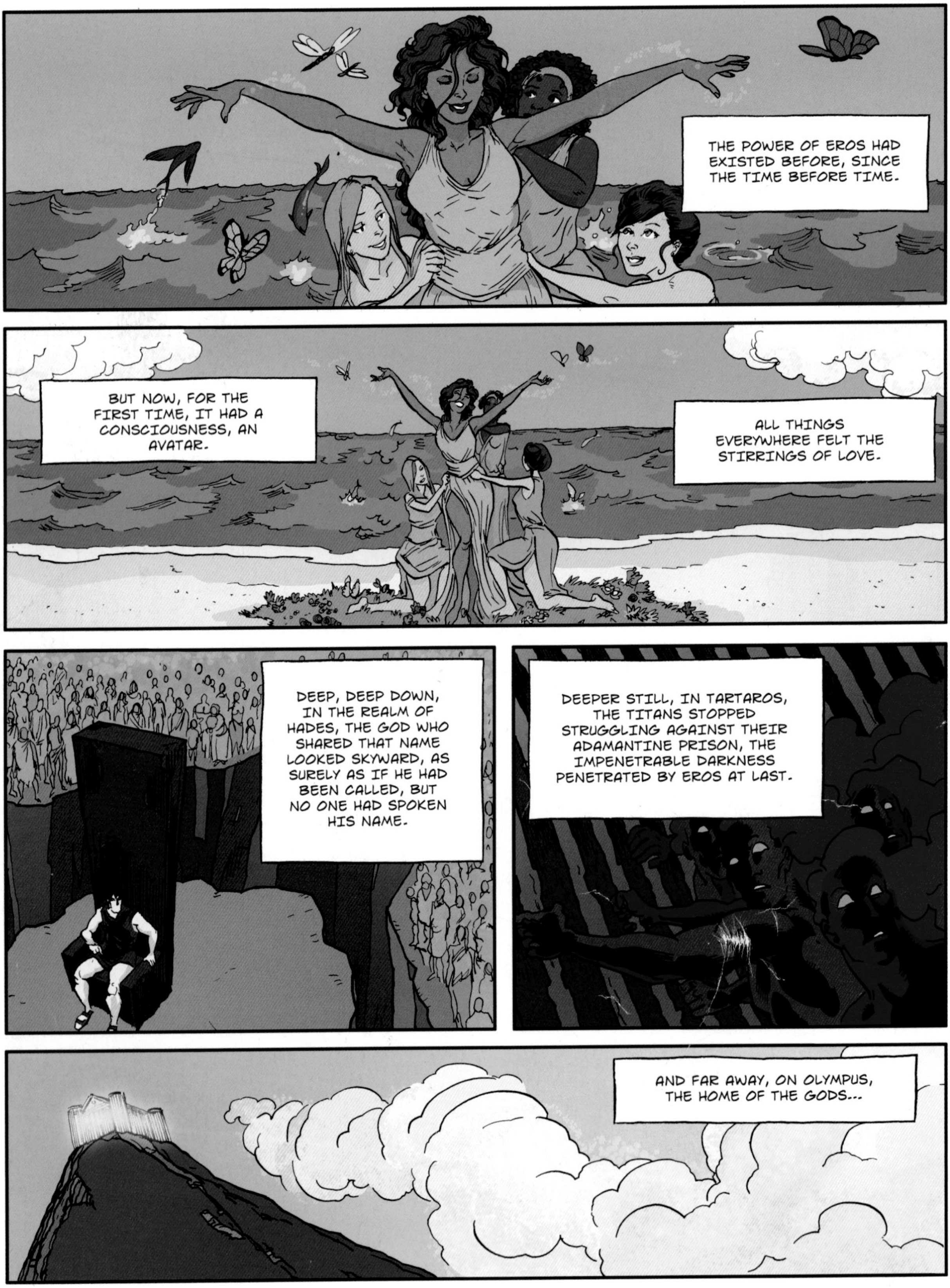
THE POWER OF EROS HAD EXISTED BEFORE, SINCE THE TIME BEFORE TIME.
BUT NOW, FOR THE FIRST TIME, IT HAD A CONSCIOUSNESS, AN AVATAR.
ALL THINGS EVERYWHERE FELT THE STIRRINGS OF LOVE.
DEEP, DEEP DOWN, IN THE REALM OF HADES, THE GOD WHO SHARED THAT NAME LOOKED SKYWARD, AS SURELY AS IF HE HAD BEEN CALLED, BUT NO ONE HAD SPOKEN HIS NAME.
DEEPER STILL, IN TARTAROS, THE TITANS STOPPED STRUGGLING AGAINST THEIR ADAMANTINE PRISON, THE IMPENETRABLE DARKNESS PENETRATED BY EROS AT LAST.
AND FAR AWAY, ON OLYMPUS, THE HOME OF THE GODS...

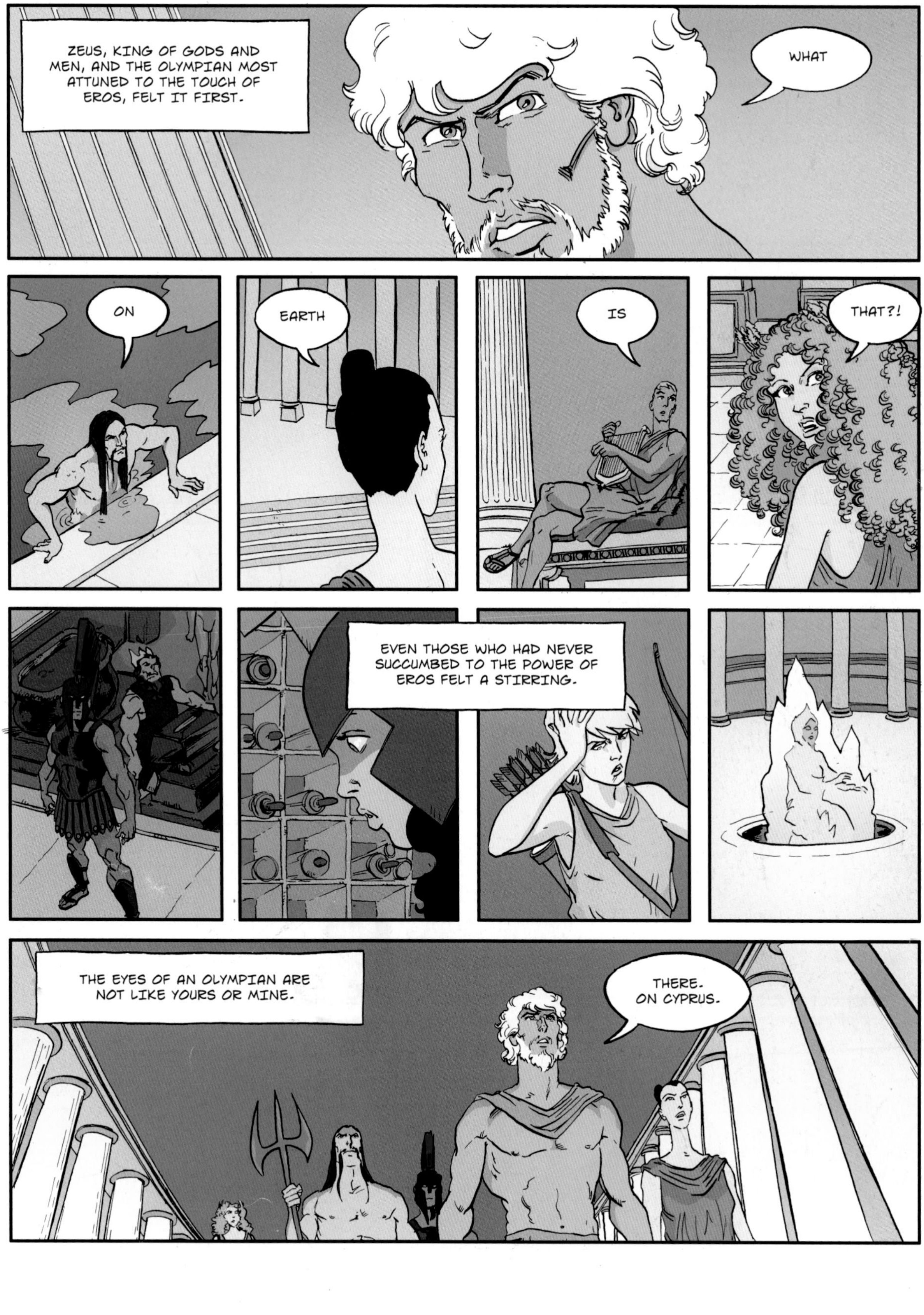
ZEUS, KING OF GODS AND MEN, AND THE OLYMPIAN MOST ATTUNED TO THE TOUCH OF EROS, FELT IT FIRST.
WHAT
ON
EARTH
IS
THAT?!
EVEN THOSE WHO HAD NEVER SUCCUMBED TO THE POWER OF EROS FELT A STIRRING.
THE EYES OF AN OLYMPIAN ARE NOT LIKE YOURS OR MINE.
THERE. ON CYPRUS.

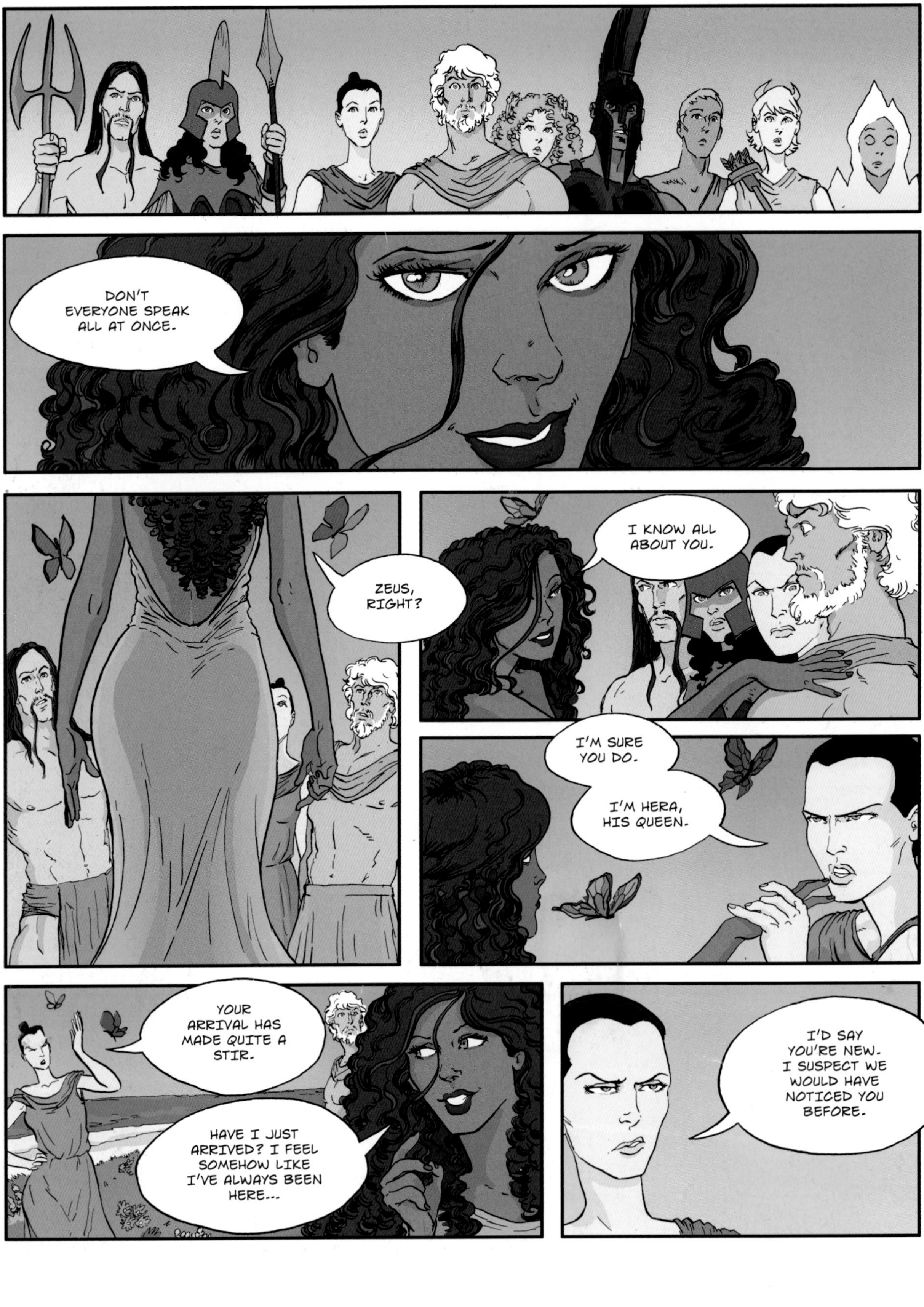
DON'T EVERYONE SPEAK ALL AT ONCE.
ZEUS, RIGHT?
I KNOW ALL ABOUT YOU.
I'M SURE YOU DO.
I'M HERA, HIS QUEEN.
YOUR ARRIVAL HAS MADE QUITE A STIR.
HAVE I JUST ARRIVED? I FEEL SOMEHOW LIKE I'VE ALWAYS BEEN HERE...
I'D SAY YOU'RE NEW. I SUSPECT WE WOULD HAVE NOTICED YOU BEFORE.

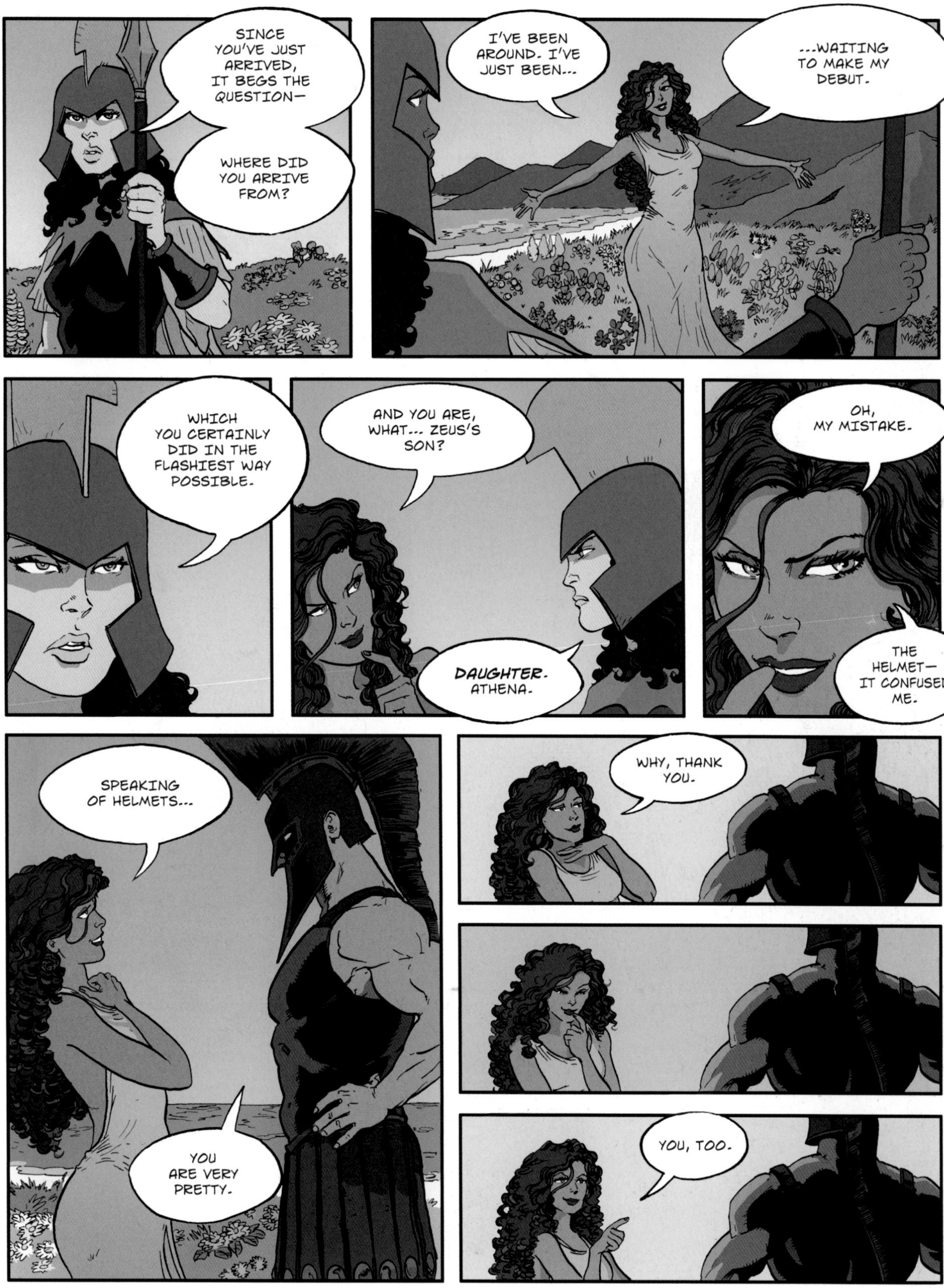
SINCE YOU'VE JUST ARRIVED, IT BEGS THE QUESTION—
WHERE DID YOU ARRIVE FROM?
I'VE BEEN AROUND. I'VE JUST BEEN...
...WAITING TO MAKE MY DEBUT.
WHICH YOU CERTAINLY DID IN THE FLASHIEST WAY POSSIBLE.
AND YOU ARE, WHAT... ZEUS'S SON?
DAUGHTER. ATHENA.
OH, MY MISTAKE.
THE HELMET— IT CONFUSED ME.
SPEAKING OF HELMETS...
YOU ARE VERY PRETTY.
WHY, THANK YOU.
YOU, TOO.

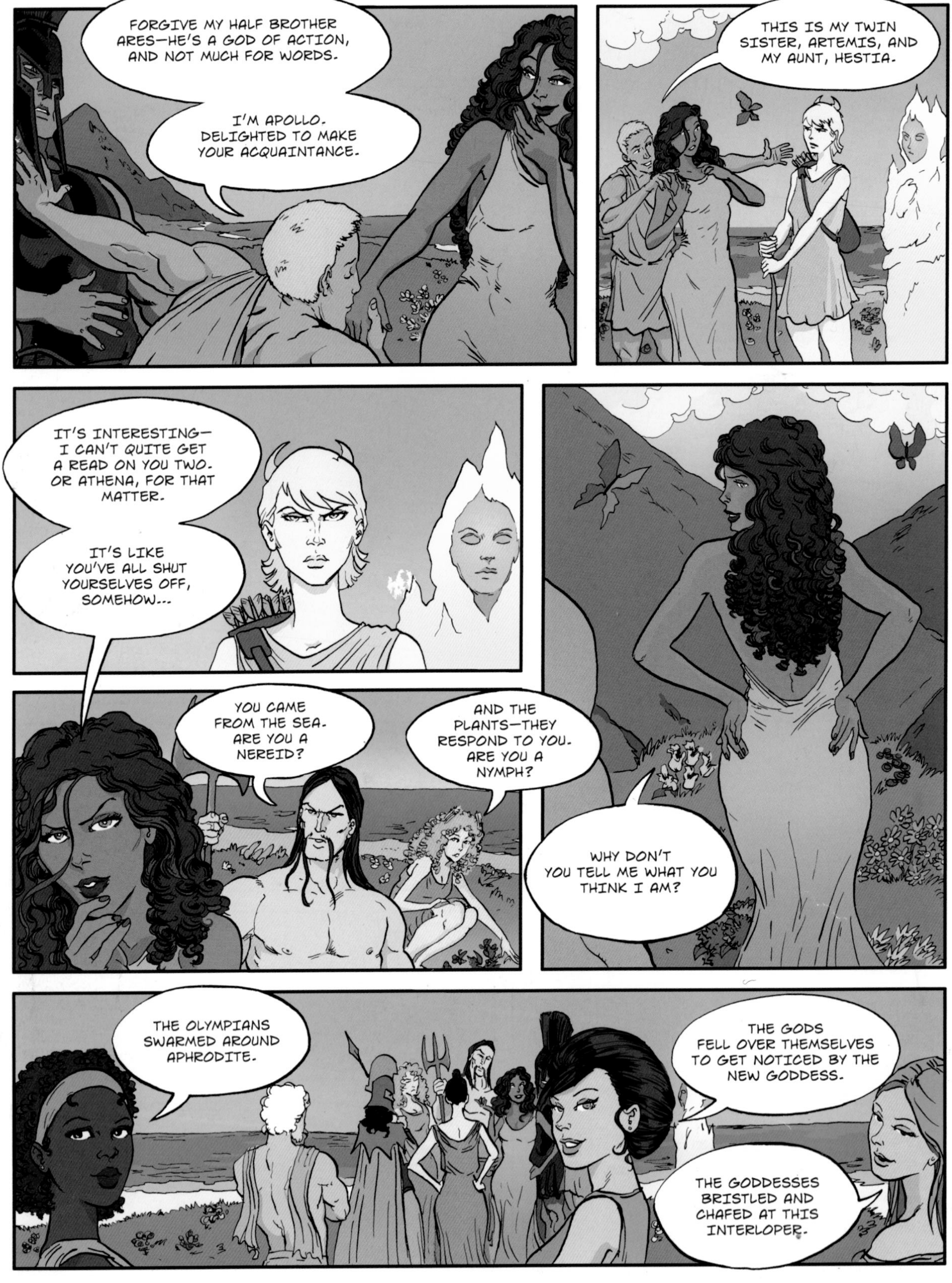
FORGIVE MY HALF BROTHER ARES—HE'S A GOD OF ACTION, AND NOT MUCH FOR WORDS.
I'M APOLLO. DELIGHTED TO MAKE YOUR ACQUAINTANCE.
THIS IS MY TWIN SISTER, ARTEMIS, AND MY AUNT, HESTIA.
IT'S INTERESTING—I CAN'T QUITE GET A READ ON YOU TWO. OR ATHENA, FOR THAT MATTER.
IT'S LIKE YOU'VE ALL SHUT YOURSELVES OFF, SOMEHOW...
YOU CAME FROM THE SEA. ARE YOU A NEREID?
AND THE PLANTS—THEY RESPOND TO YOU. ARE YOU A NYMPH?
WHY DON'T YOU TELL ME WHAT YOU THINK I AM?
THE OLYMPIANS SWARMED AROUND APHRODITE.
THE GODS FELL OVER THEMSELVES TO GET NOTICED BY THE NEW GODDESS.
THE GODDESSES BRISTLED AND CHAFED AT THIS INTERLOPER.

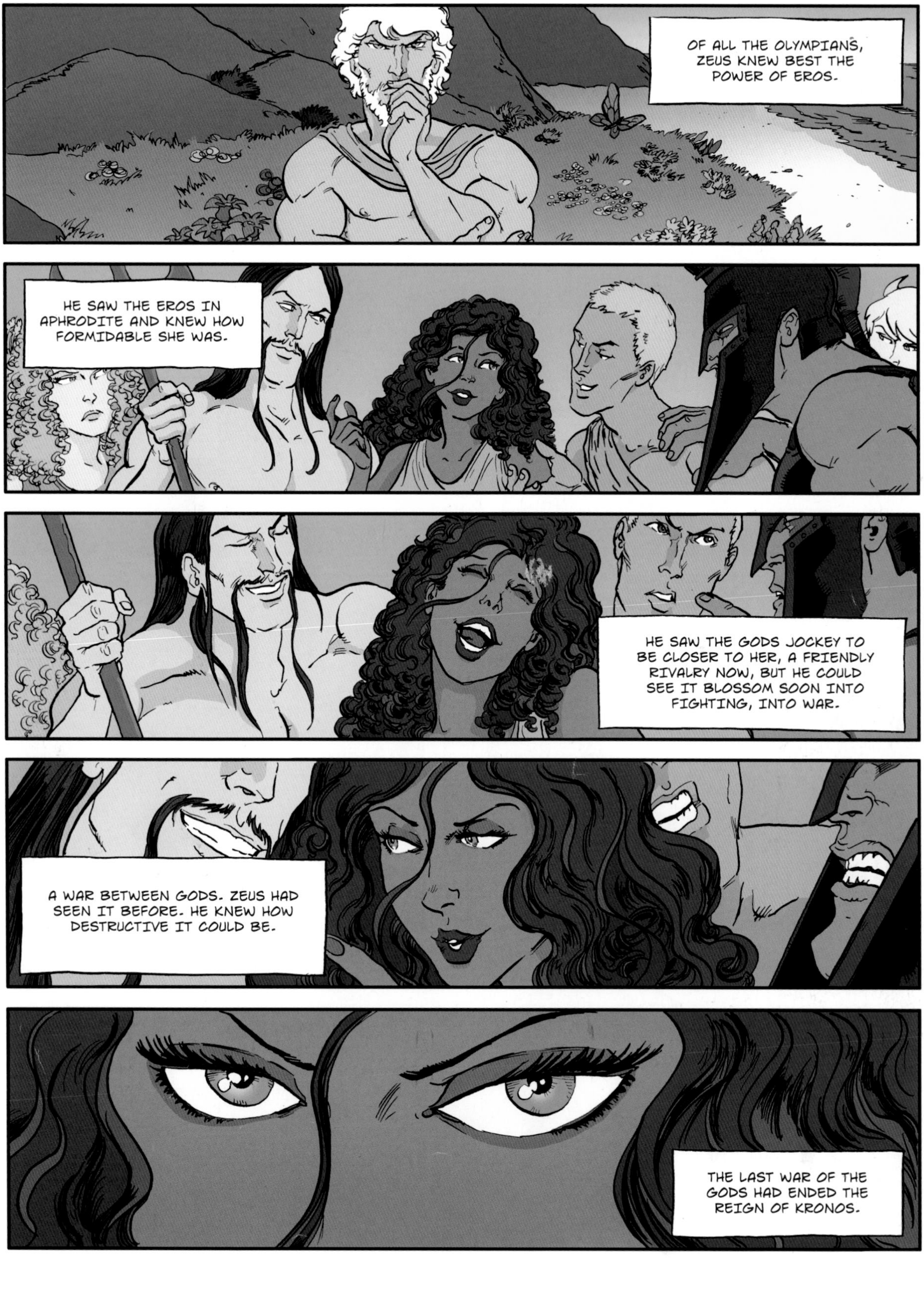
OF ALL THE OLYMPIANS, ZEUS KNEW BEST THE POWER OF EROS.
HE SAW THE EROS IN APHRODITE AND KNEW HOW FORMIDABLE SHE WAS.
HE SAW THE GODS JOCKEY TO BE CLOSER TO HER, A FRIENDLY RIVALRY NOW, BUT HE COULD SEE IT BLOSSOM SOON INTO FIGHTING, INTO WAR.
A WAR BETWEEN GODS. ZEUS HAD SEEN IT BEFORE. HE KNEW HOW DESTRUCTIVE IT COULD BE.
THE LAST WAR OF THE GODS HAD ENDED THE REIGN OF KRONOS.

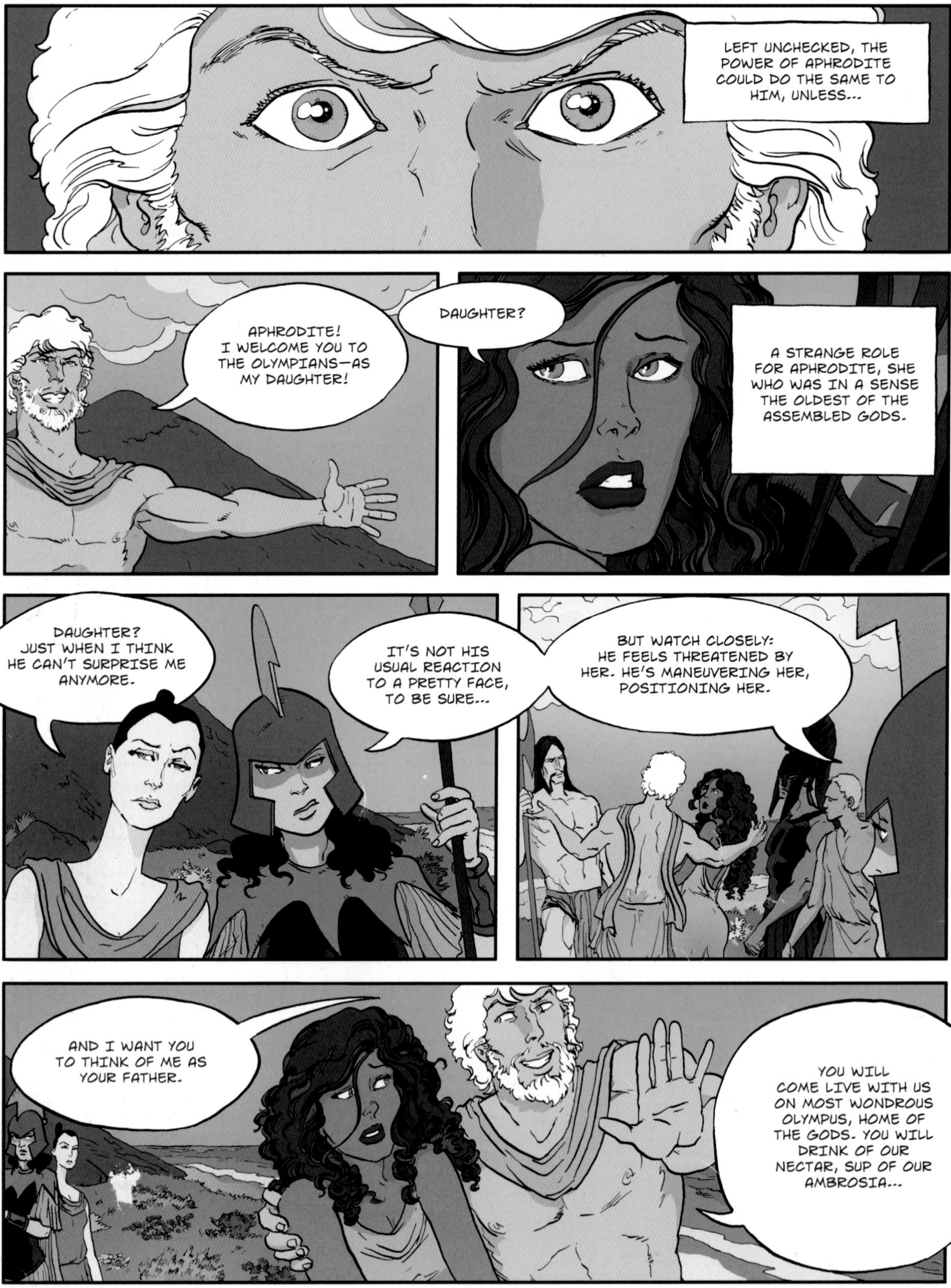
LEFT UNCHECKED, THE POWER OF APHRODITE COULD DO THE SAME TO HIM, UNLESS...
APHRODITE! I WELCOME YOU TO THE OLYMPIANS—AS MY DAUGHTER!
DAUGHTER?
A STRANGE ROLE FOR APHRODITE, SHE WHO WAS IN A SENSE THE OLDEST OF THE ASSEMBLED GODS.
DAUGHTER? JUST WHEN I THINK HE CAN'T SURPRISE ME ANYMORE.
IT'S NOT HIS USUAL REACTION TO A PRETTY FACE, TO BE SURE...
BUT WATCH CLOSELY: HE FEELS THREATENED BY HER. HE'S MANEUVERING HER, POSITIONING HER.
AND I WANT YOU TO THINK OF ME AS YOUR FATHER.
YOU WILL COME LIVE WITH US ON MOST WONDROUS OLYMPUS, HOME OF THE GODS. YOU WILL DRINK OF OUR NECTAR, SUP OF OUR AMBROSIA...

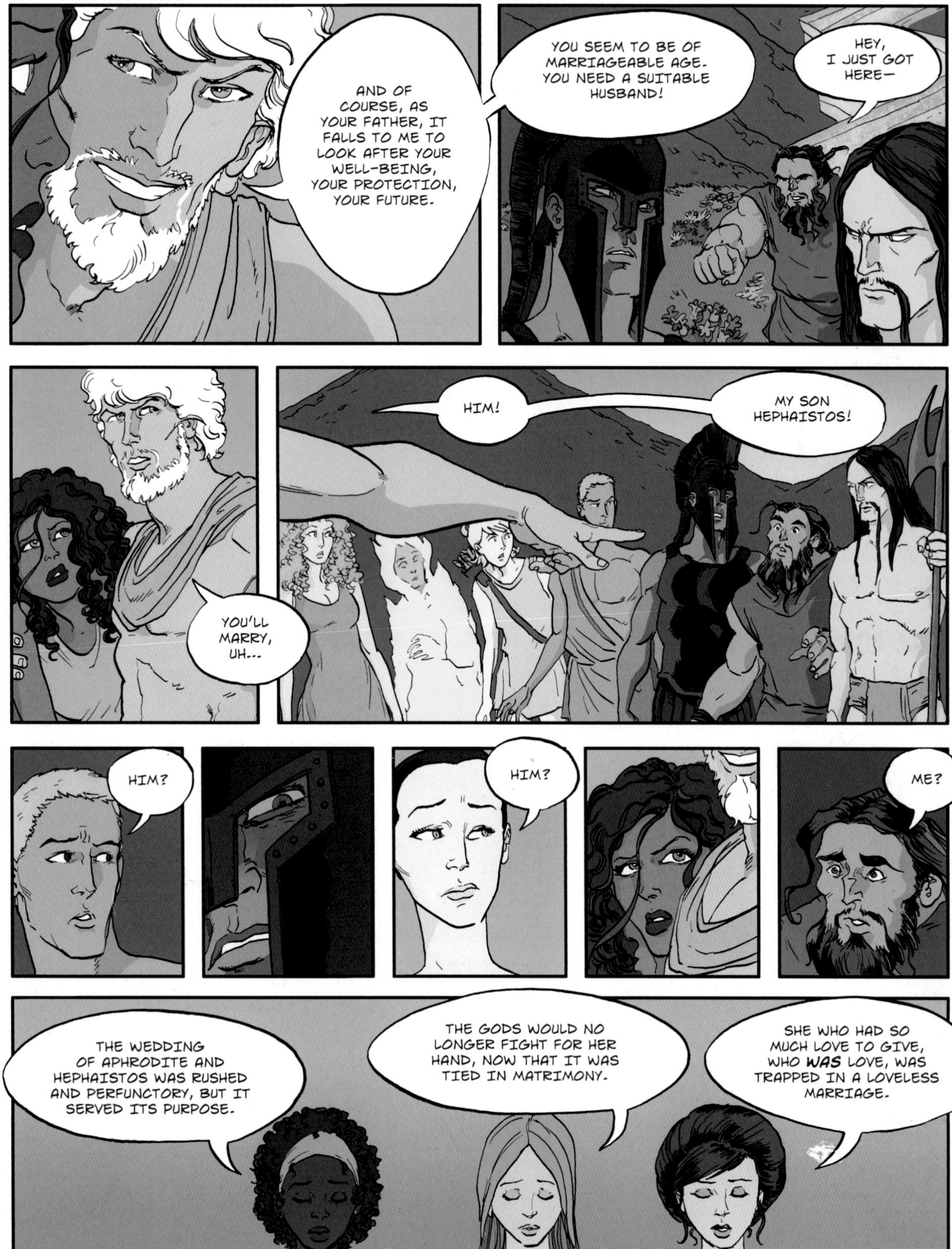
AND OF COURSE, AS YOUR FATHER, IT FALLS TO ME TO LOOK AFTER YOUR WELL-BEING, YOUR PROTECTION, YOUR FUTURE.
YOU SEEM TO BE OF MARRIAGEABLE AGE. YOU NEED A SUITABLE HUSBAND!
HEY, I JUST GOT HERE—
YOU'LL MARRY, UH...
HIM!
MY SON HEPHAISTOS!
HIM?
HIM?
ME?
THE WEDDING OF APHRODITE AND HEPHAISTOS WAS RUSHED AND PERFUNCTORY, BUT IT SERVED ITS PURPOSE.
THE GODS WOULD NO LONGER FIGHT FOR HER HAND, NOW THAT IT WAS TIED IN MATRIMONY.
SHE WHO HAD SO MUCH LOVE TO GIVE, WHO WAS LOVE, WAS TRAPPED IN A LOVELESS MARRIAGE.

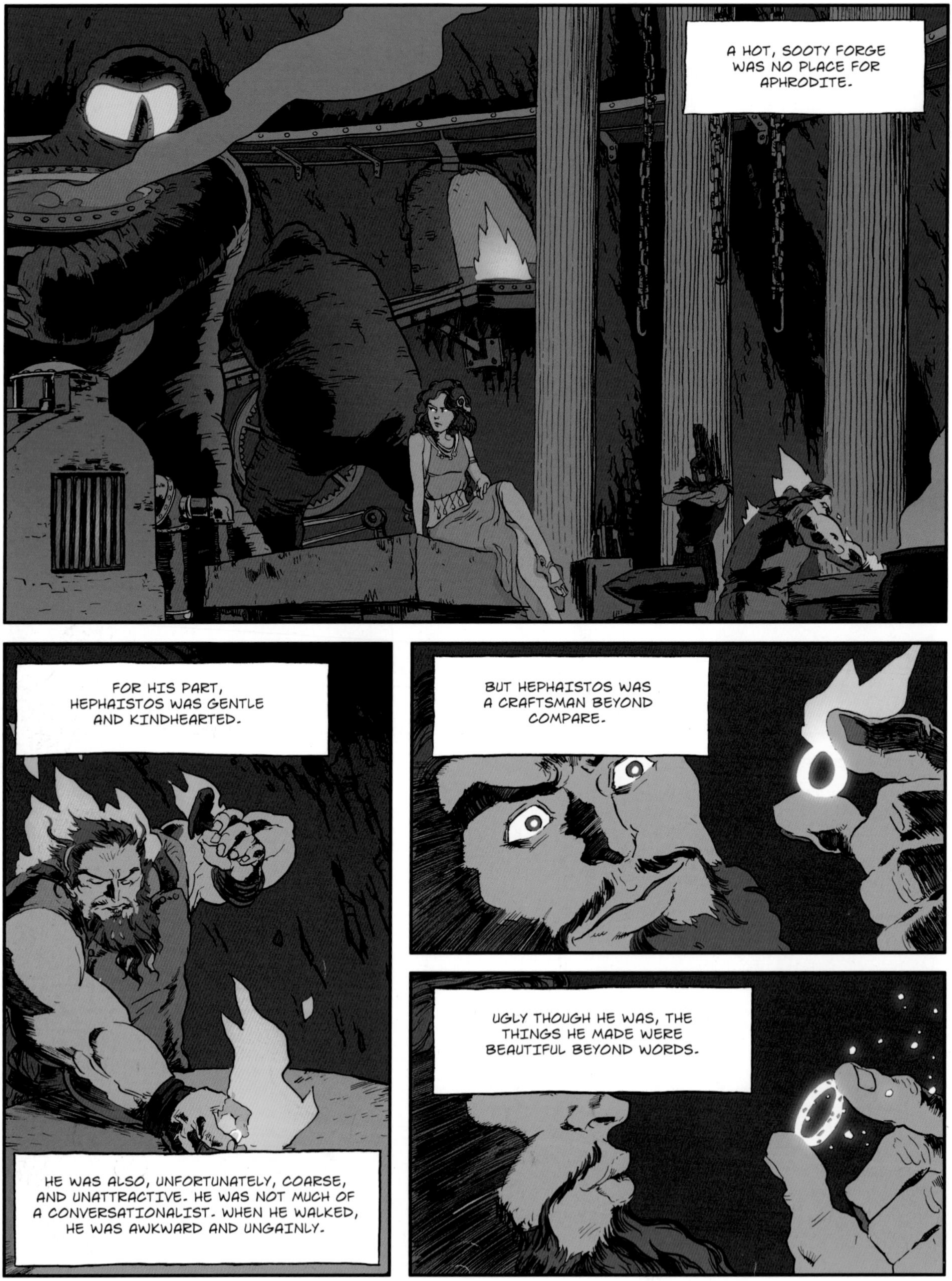
A HOT, SOOTY FORGE WAS NO PLACE FOR APHRODITE.
FOR HIS PART, HEPHAISTOS WAS GENTLE AND KINDHEARTED.
HE WAS ALSO, UNFORTUNATELY, COARSE, AND UNATTRACTIVE. HE WAS NOT MUCH OF A CONVERSATIONALIST. WHEN HE WALKED, HE WAS AWKWARD AND UNGAINLY.
BUT HEPHAISTOS WAS A CRAFTSMAN BEYOND COMPARE.
UGLY THOUGH HE WAS, THE THINGS HE MADE WERE BEAUTIFUL BEYOND WORDS.

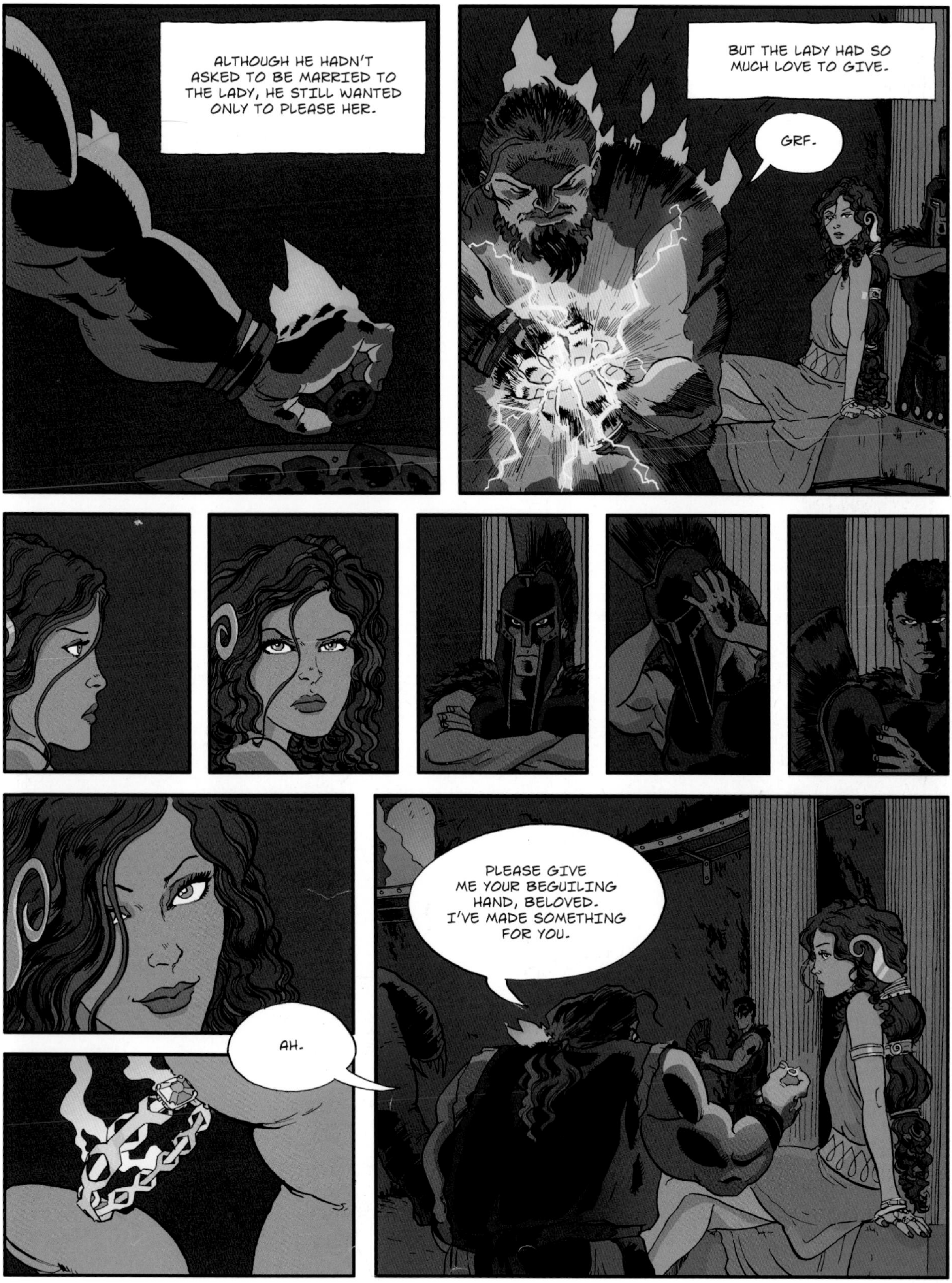

ALTHOUGH HE HADN'T ASKED TO BE MARRIED TO THE LADY, HE STILL WANTED ONLY TO PLEASE HER.
BUT THE LADY HAD SO MUCH LOVE TO GIVE.
GRF.
PLEASE GIVE ME YOUR BEGUILING HAND, BELOVED. I'VE MADE SOMETHING FOR YOU.
AH.

IT'S VERY STUFFY IN HERE. I'M GOING TO GO FOR A WALK.

TAKE CARE, BELOVED!

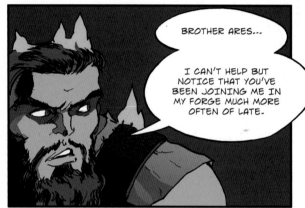

BROTHER ARES...

I CAN'T HELP BUT NOTICE THAT YOU'VE BEEN JOINING ME IN MY FORGE MUCH MORE OFTEN OF LATE.

YOU CRAFT THE SHARPEST BLADES.

AND THERE IS NO SHORTAGE OF WARS IN THE WORLD.

POOR, POOR APHRODITE.

SO ALONE! SO UNHAPPY!

IF ONLY WE COULD DO SOMETHING FOR HER!

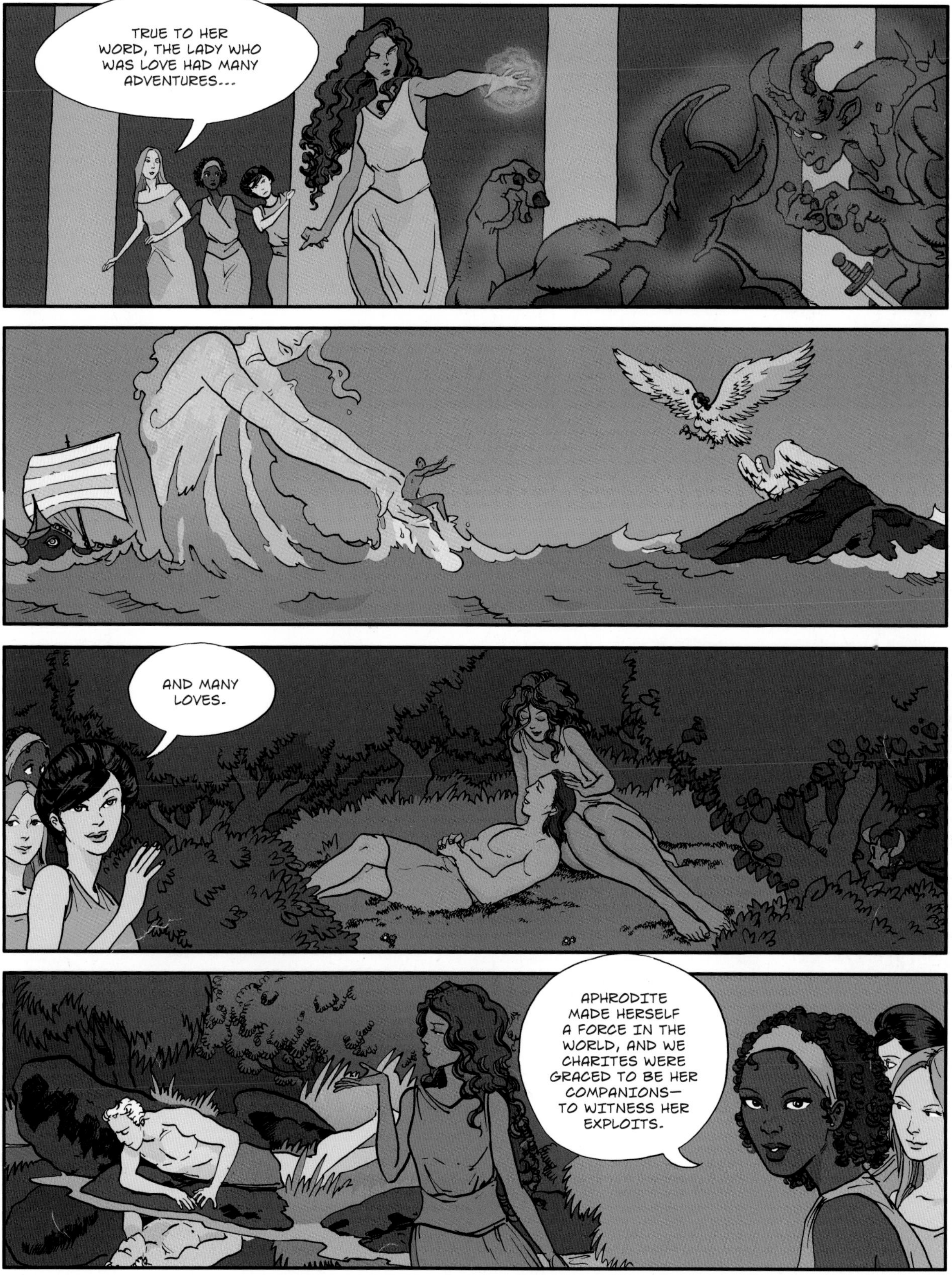
TRUE TO HER WORD, THE LADY WHO WAS LOVE HAD MANY ADVENTURES...
AND MANY LOVES.
APHRODITE MADE HERSELF A FORCE IN THE WORLD, AND WE CHARITES WERE GRACED TO BE HER COMPANIONS— TO WITNESS HER EXPLOITS.

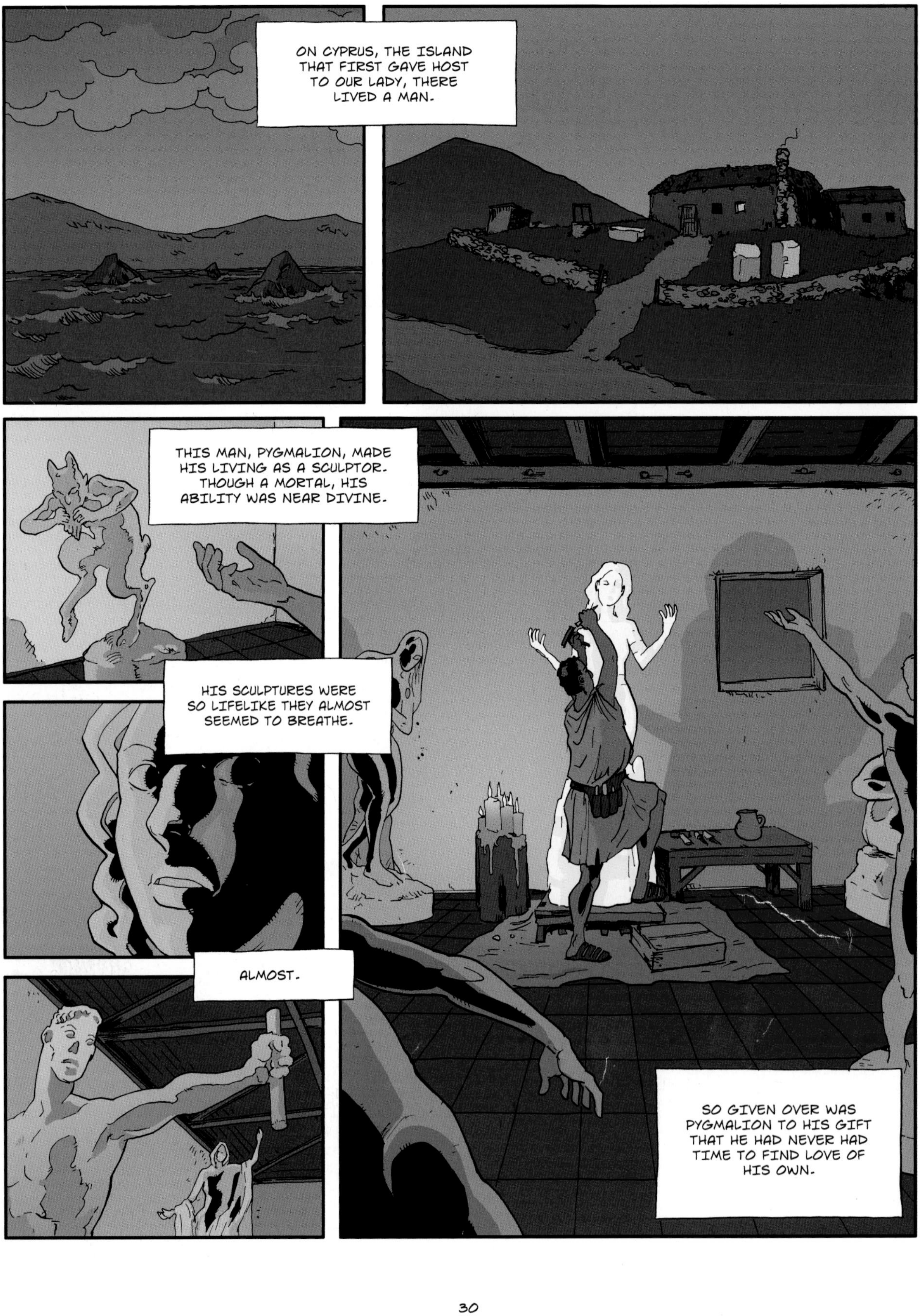
ON CYPRUS, THE ISLAND THAT FIRST GAVE HOST TO OUR LADY, THERE LIVED A MAN.
THIS MAN, PYGMALION, MADE HIS LIVING AS A SCULPTOR. THOUGH A MORTAL, HIS ABILITY WAS NEAR DIVINE.
HIS SCULPTURES WERE SO LIFELIKE THEY ALMOST SEEMED TO BREATHE.
ALMOST.
SO GIVEN OVER WAS PYGMALION TO HIS GIFT THAT HE HAD NEVER HAD TIME TO FIND LOVE OF HIS OWN.

HE WAS LONELY, BUT NEVER REALIZED IT.

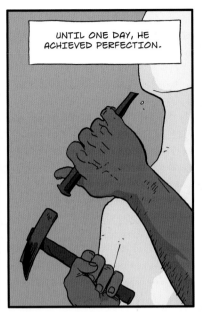

UNTIL ONE DAY, HE ACHIEVED PERFECTION.

AN IVORY STATUE OF OUR LADY, APHRODITE.

PYGMALION LOOKED UPON HIS CREATION, AND HIS HEART SWELLED WITH LOVE.

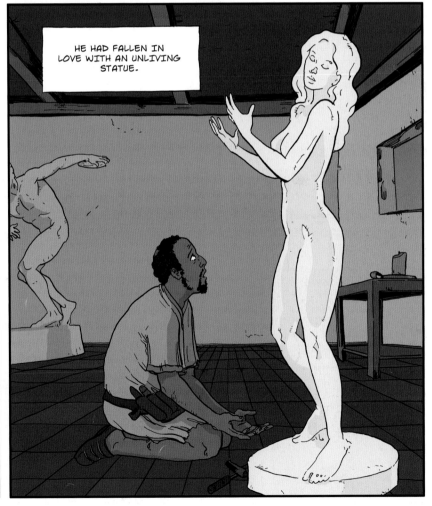

HE HAD FALLEN IN LOVE WITH AN UNLIVING STATUE.

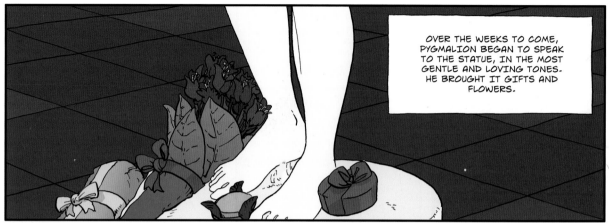

OVER THE WEEKS TO COME, PYGMALION BEGAN TO SPEAK TO THE STATUE, IN THE MOST GENTLE AND LOVING TONES. HE BROUGHT IT GIFTS AND FLOWERS.

EACH DAY PYGMALION DRESSED THE STATUE IN DIFFERENT BEAUTIFUL ROBES.

HE ADORNED ITS DELICATE HANDS WITH ORNAMENTS AND JEWELRY.

HE APPLIED MAKEUP TO ITS FACE, UNTIL IT SEEMED ALMOST ALIVE, ALMOST BREATHING.

ALMOST.

AT NIGHT, PYGMALION WOULD LAY THE STATUE ON A BED OF SILK SHEETS AND SOFT PILLOWS, AS IF IT NEEDED REST.

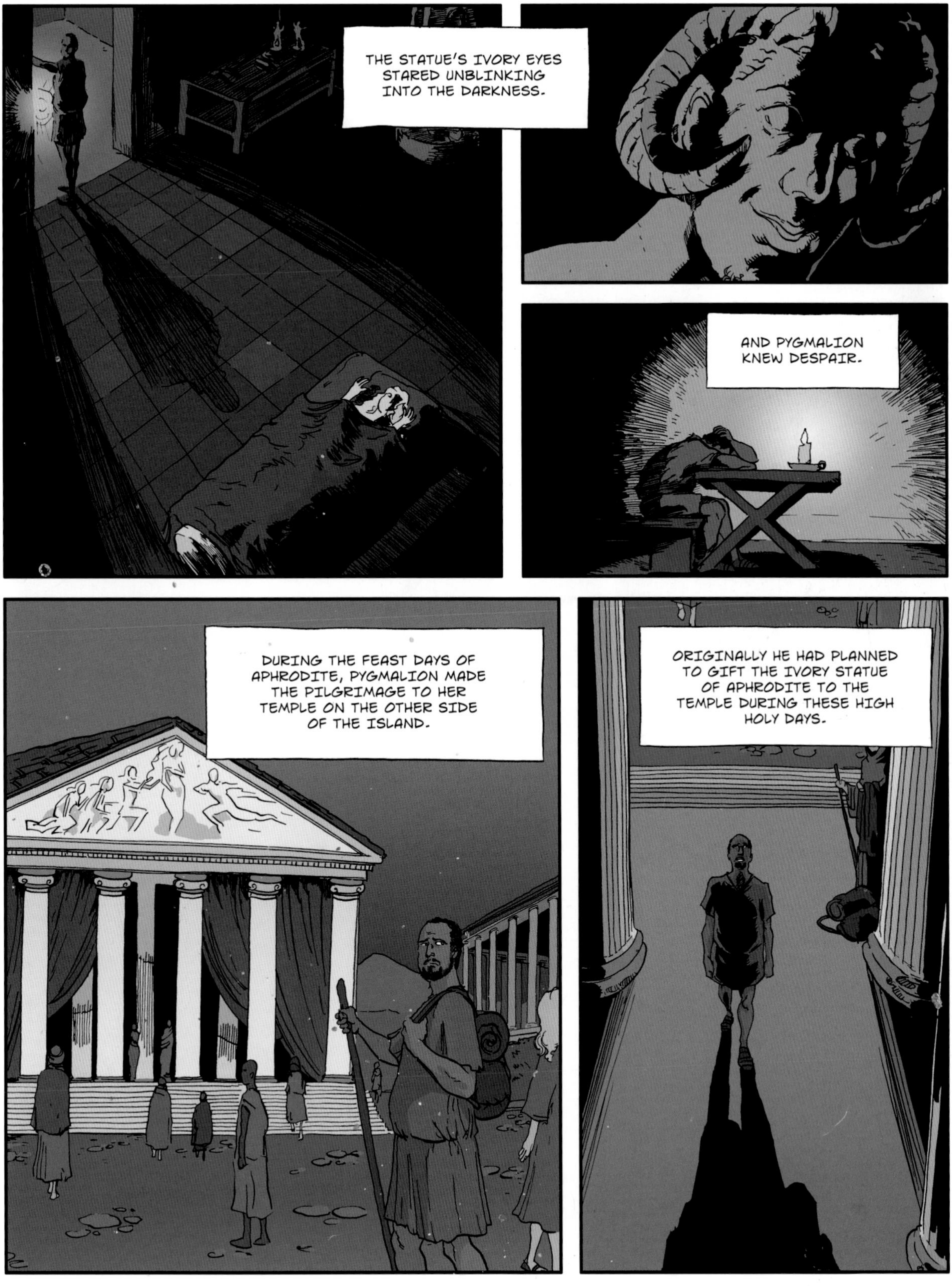
THE STATUE'S IVORY EYES STARED UNBLINKING INTO THE DARKNESS.
AND PYGMALION KNEW DESPAIR.
DURING THE FEAST DAYS OF APHRODITE, PYGMALION MADE THE PILGRIMAGE TO HER TEMPLE ON THE OTHER SIDE OF THE ISLAND.
ORIGINALLY HE HAD PLANNED TO GIFT THE IVORY STATUE OF APHRODITE TO THE TEMPLE DURING THESE HIGH HOLY DAYS.

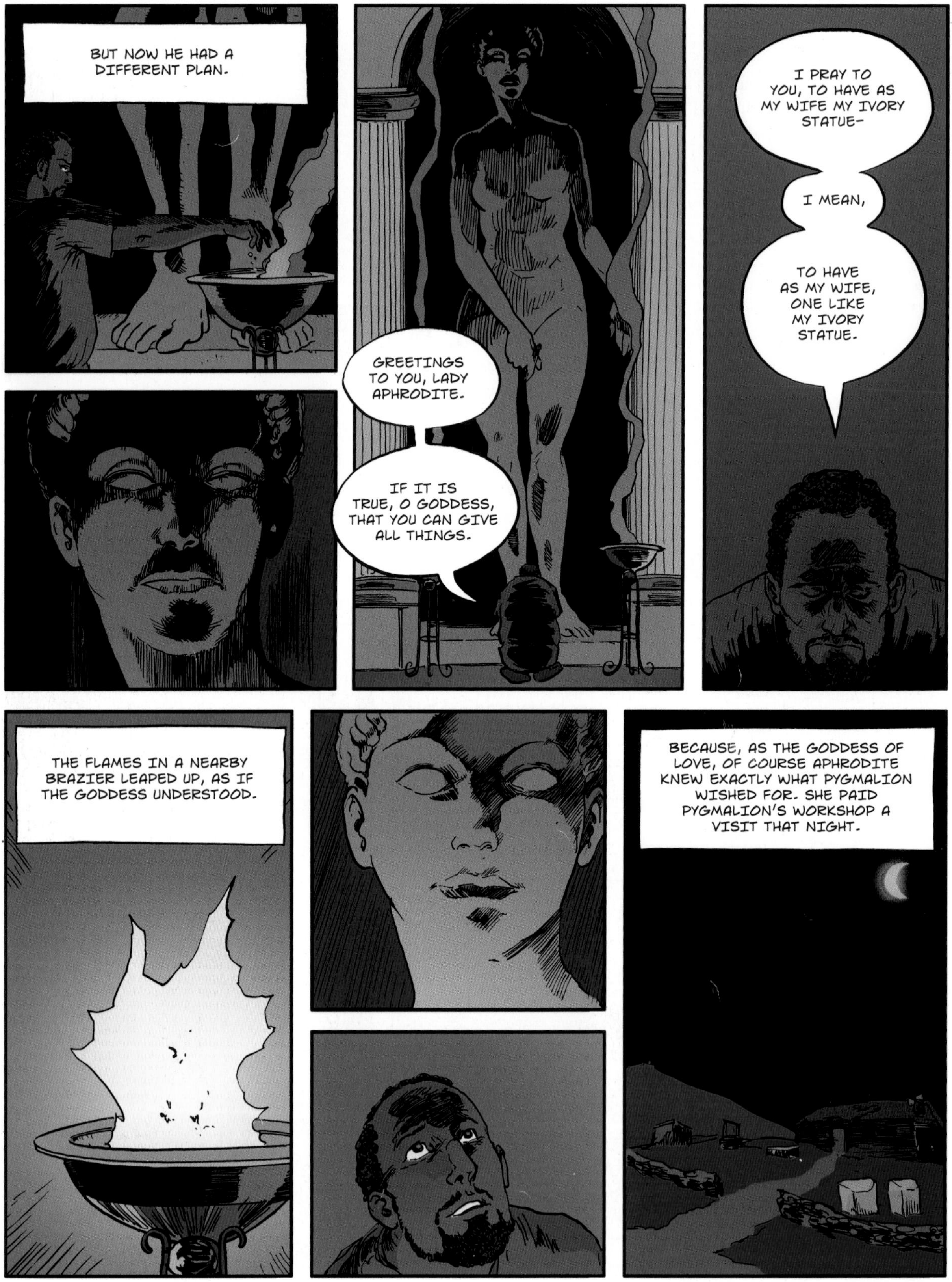
BUT NOW HE HAD A DIFFERENT PLAN.
GREETINGS TO YOU, LADY APHRODITE.
IF IT IS TRUE, O GODDESS, THAT YOU CAN GIVE ALL THINGS.
I PRAY TO YOU, TO HAVE AS MY WIFE MY IVORY STATUE-
I MEAN,
TO HAVE AS MY WIFE, ONE LIKE MY IVORY STATUE.
THE FLAMES IN A NEARBY BRAZIER LEAPED UP, AS IF THE GODDESS UNDERSTOOD.
BECAUSE, AS THE GODDESS OF LOVE, OF COURSE APHRODITE KNEW EXACTLY WHAT PYGMALION WISHED FOR. SHE PAID PYGMALION'S WORKSHOP A VISIT THAT NIGHT.

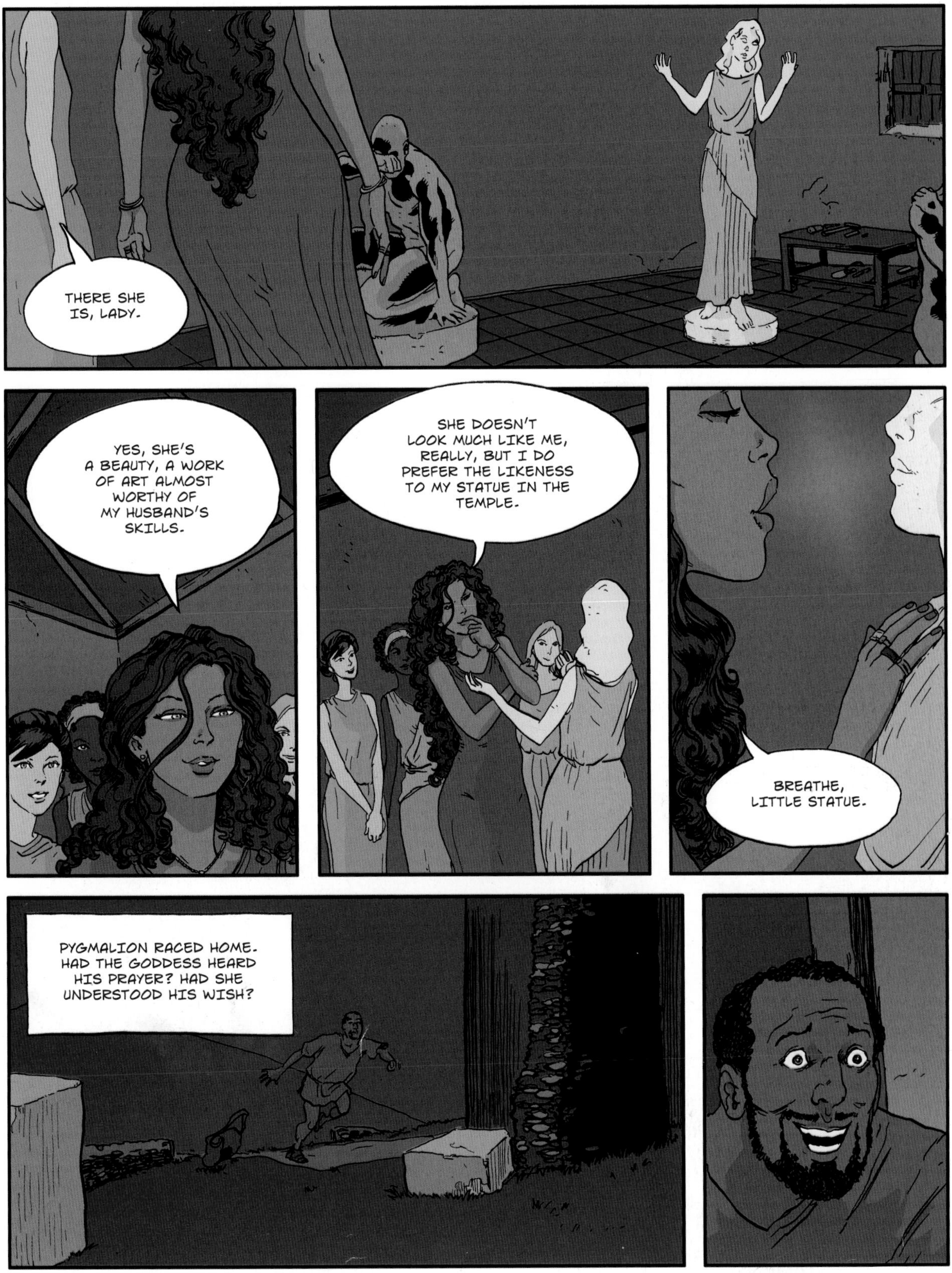
THERE SHE IS, LADY.
YES, SHE'S A BEAUTY, A WORK OF ART ALMOST WORTHY OF MY HUSBAND'S SKILLS.
SHE DOESN'T LOOK MUCH LIKE ME, REALLY, BUT I DO PREFER THE LIKENESS TO MY STATUE IN THE TEMPLE.
BREATHE, LITTLE STATUE.
PYGMALION RACED HOME. HAD THE GODDESS HEARD HIS PRAYER? HAD SHE UNDERSTOOD HIS WISH?

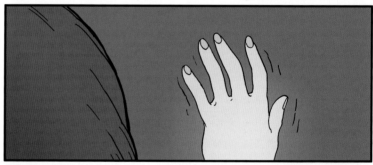

PYGMALION AND GALATEA (FOR THAT WAS THE NAME THE NOW–LIVING STATUE TOOK FOR HERSELF) WERE WED IN THE FALL.

IT WAS A GRAND AFFAIR, FOR PYGMALION'S GIFTS HAD MADE HIM A WEALTHY MAN, AND HE INVITED THE ENTIRE TOWN.

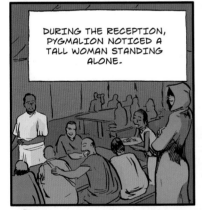

DURING THE RECEPTION, PYGMALION NOTICED A TALL WOMAN STANDING ALONE.

HELLO, UH, I DON'T THINK I KNOW YOU, BUT I FEEL, SOMEHOW...

LIKE WE OUGHT TO THANK YOU?

THERE IS NOTHING TO THANK ME FOR.

LOVE LIKE YOUR HUSBAND HAS IS LOVE THAT MUST BE SHARED.

BE HAPPY TOGETHER.

YOU WERE MADE FOR EACH OTHER.

AT SOME POINT, APHRODITE HAD A CHILD, A SON.

HE SEEMED TO ARRIVE SUDDENLY, WITHOUT WARNING, AND THEN IT WAS IF HE HAD ALWAYS BEEN THERE. HIS MOTHER'S CONSTANT COMPANION.

HIS ARRIVAL WAS SO MYSTERIOUS, EVEN THE IDENTITY OF HIS FATHER WAS A SECRET.

APHRODITE'S HUSBAND WOULD SEEM THE LIKELY CHOICE.

BUT THE CHILD WAS SO BEAUTIFUL AND FAIR THAT EVEN HEPHAISTOS EXPRESSED DOUBT THAT HE COULD BE THE FATHER.

SOME THOUGHT THE FATHER WAS HERMES, AND IN FACT THE CHILD SEEMED TO SHARE CERTAIN PHYSICAL ATTRIBUTES WITH THE SWIFT-FOOTED GOD OF THIEVES AND LIARS.

OTHERS SUSPECTED ARES, GOD OF WAR, AS THE FATHER, FOR THE CHILD SHARED HIS MEAN STREAK AND A CERTAIN, SIMILAR MARTIAL QUALITY.

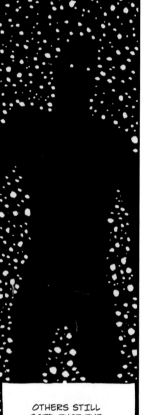

OTHERS STILL SAID THAT THE CHILD HAD BEEN BROUGHT INTO BEING AT THE SAME TIME AS HIS MOTHER, OR THAT SHE WAS LITERALLY BORN PREGNANT, AND THAT HIS FATHER WAS THUSLY OURANOS HIMSELF.

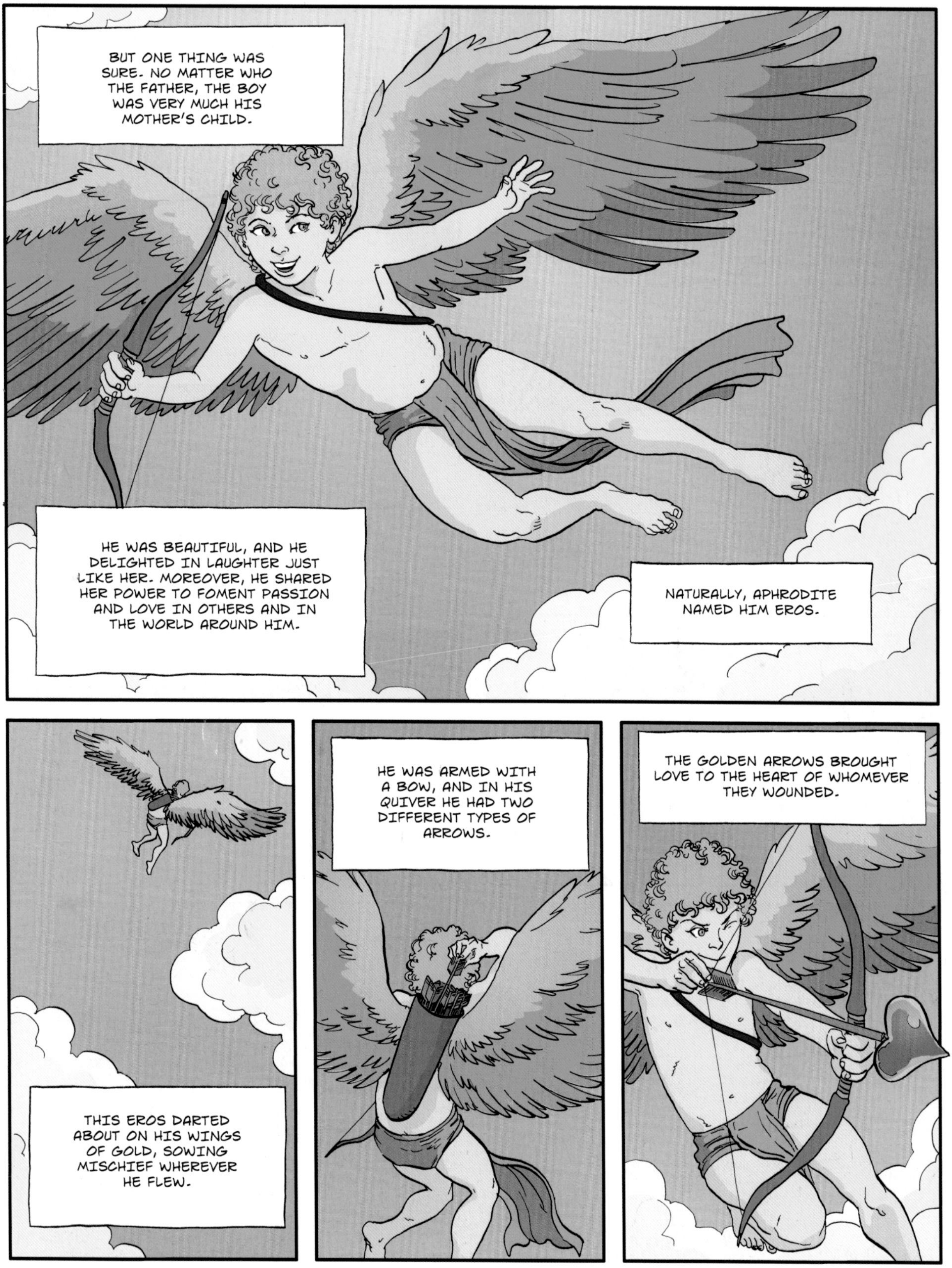
BUT ONE THING WAS SURE. NO MATTER WHO THE FATHER, THE BOY WAS VERY MUCH HIS MOTHER'S CHILD.
HE WAS BEAUTIFUL, AND HE DELIGHTED IN LAUGHTER JUST LIKE HER. MOREOVER, HE SHARED HER POWER TO FOMENT PASSION AND LOVE IN OTHERS AND IN THE WORLD AROUND HIM.
NATURALLY, APHRODITE NAMED HIM EROS.
THIS EROS DARTED ABOUT ON HIS WINGS OF GOLD, SOWING MISCHIEF WHEREVER HE FLEW.
HE WAS ARMED WITH A BOW, AND IN HIS QUIVER HE HAD TWO DIFFERENT TYPES OF ARROWS.
THE GOLDEN ARROWS BROUGHT LOVE TO THE HEART OF WHOMEVER THEY WOUNDED.

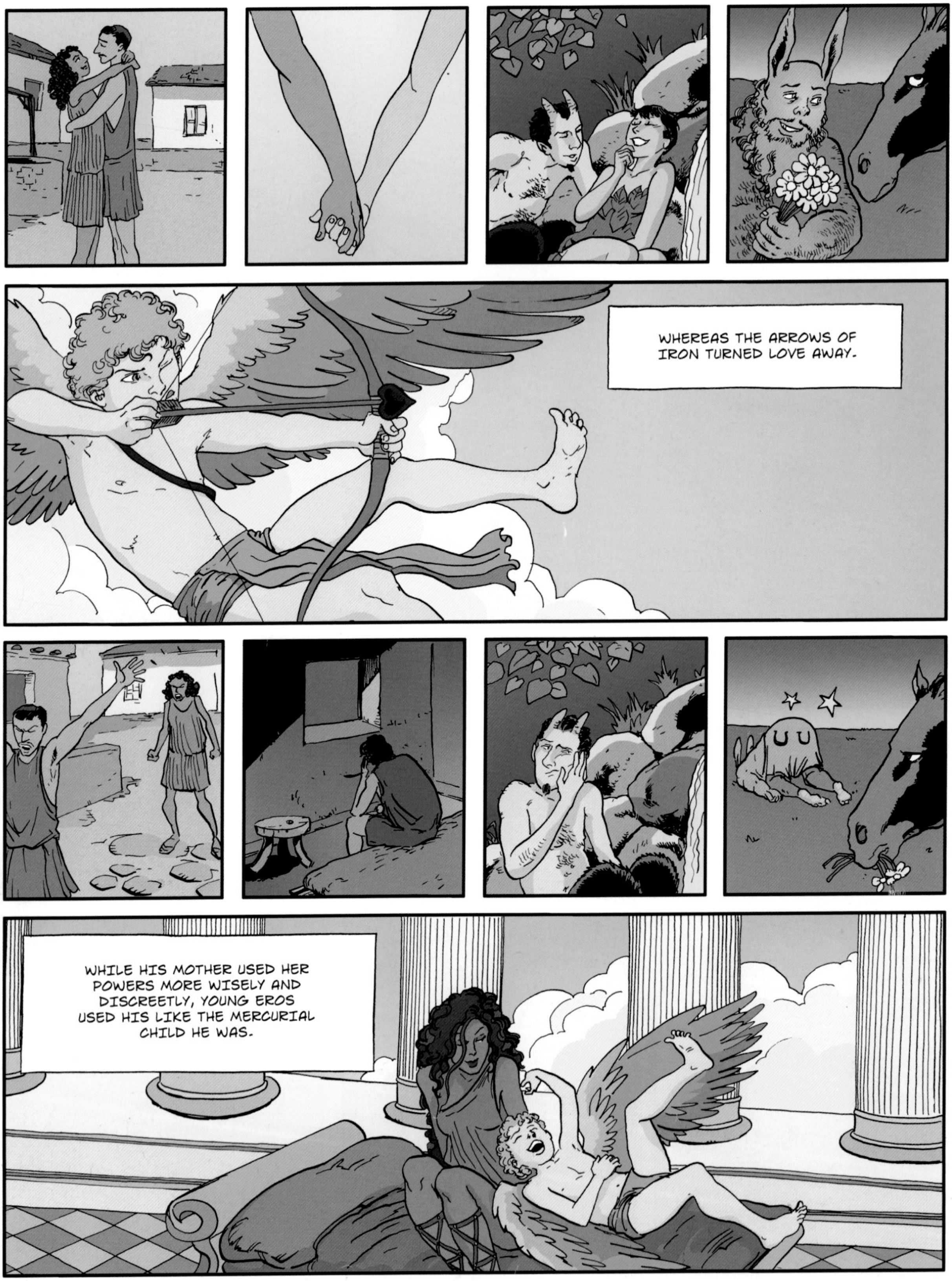
WHEREAS THE ARROWS OF IRON TURNED LOVE AWAY.
WHILE HIS MOTHER USED HER POWERS MORE WISELY AND DISCREETLY, YOUNG EROS USED HIS LIKE THE MERCURIAL CHILD HE WAS.

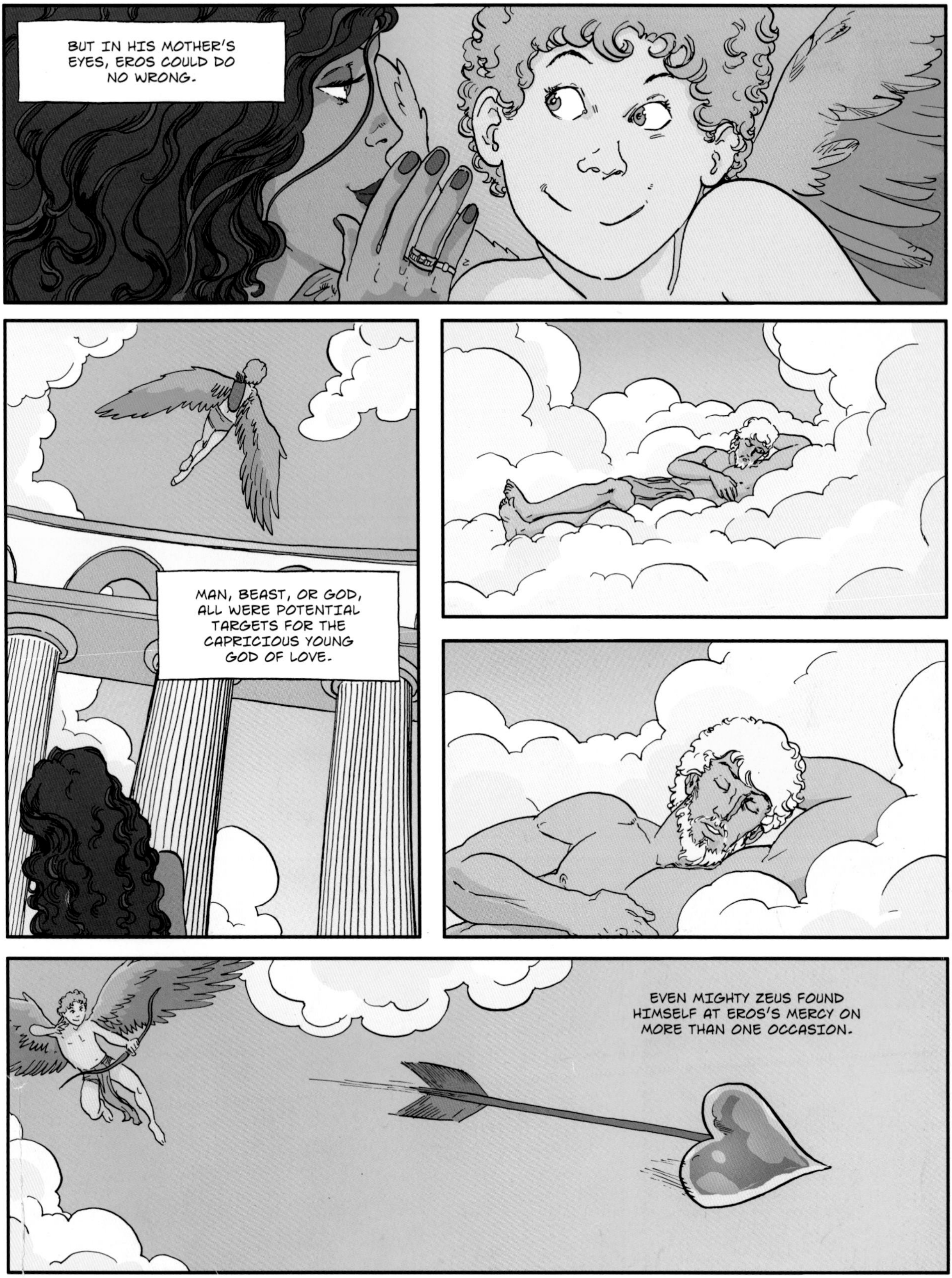
BUT IN HIS MOTHER'S EYES, EROS COULD DO NO WRONG.
MAN, BEAST, OR GOD, ALL WERE POTENTIAL TARGETS FOR THE CAPRICIOUS YOUNG GOD OF LOVE.
EVEN MIGHTY ZEUS FOUND HIMSELF AT EROS'S MERCY ON MORE THAN ONE OCCASION.

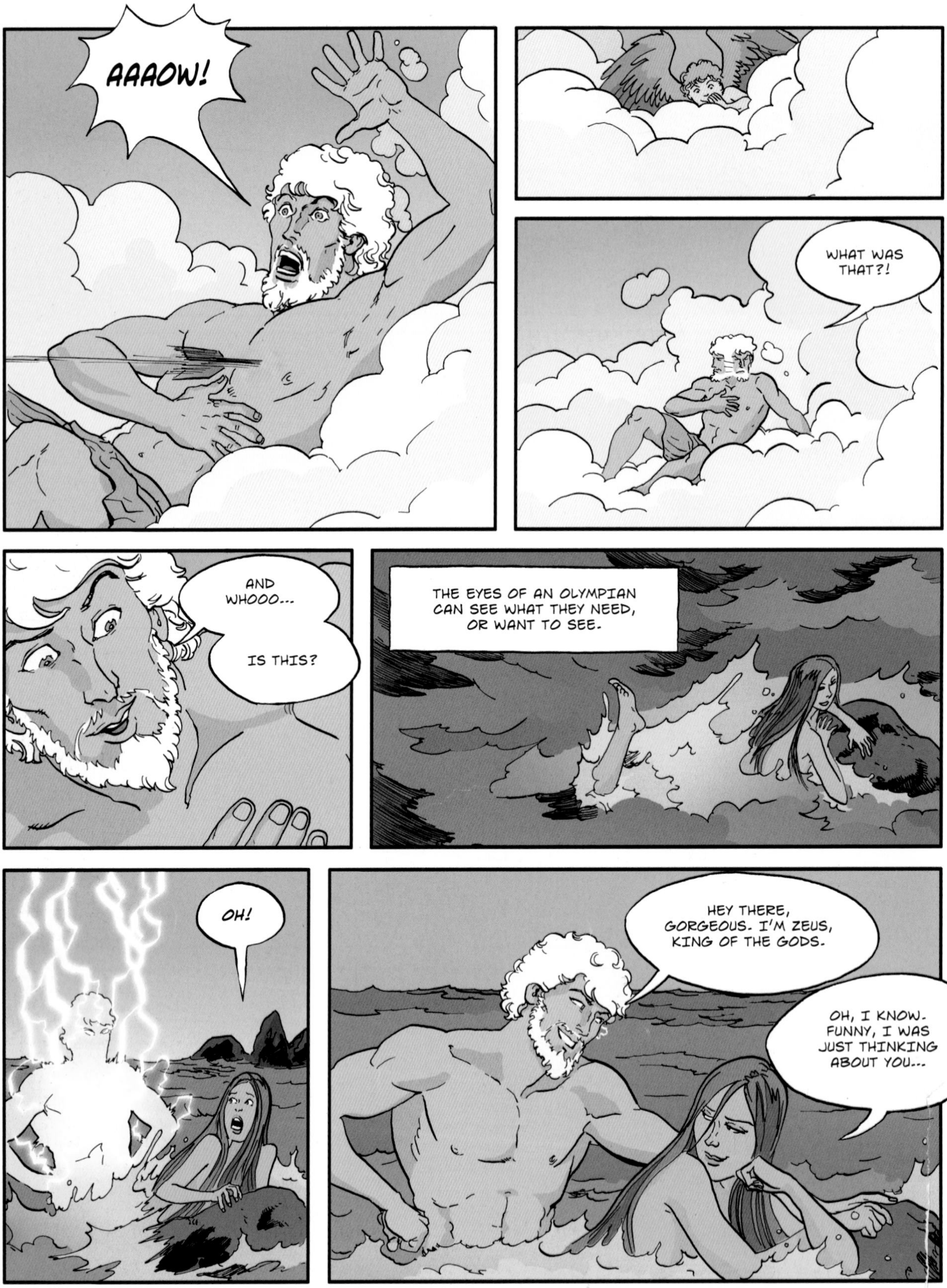
AAAOW!
WHAT WAS THAT?!
AND WHOOO...
IS THIS?
THE EYES OF AN OLYMPIAN CAN SEE WHAT THEY NEED, OR WANT TO SEE.
OH!
HEY THERE, GORGEOUS. I'M ZEUS, KING OF THE GODS.
OH, I KNOW. FUNNY, I WAS JUST THINKING ABOUT YOU...

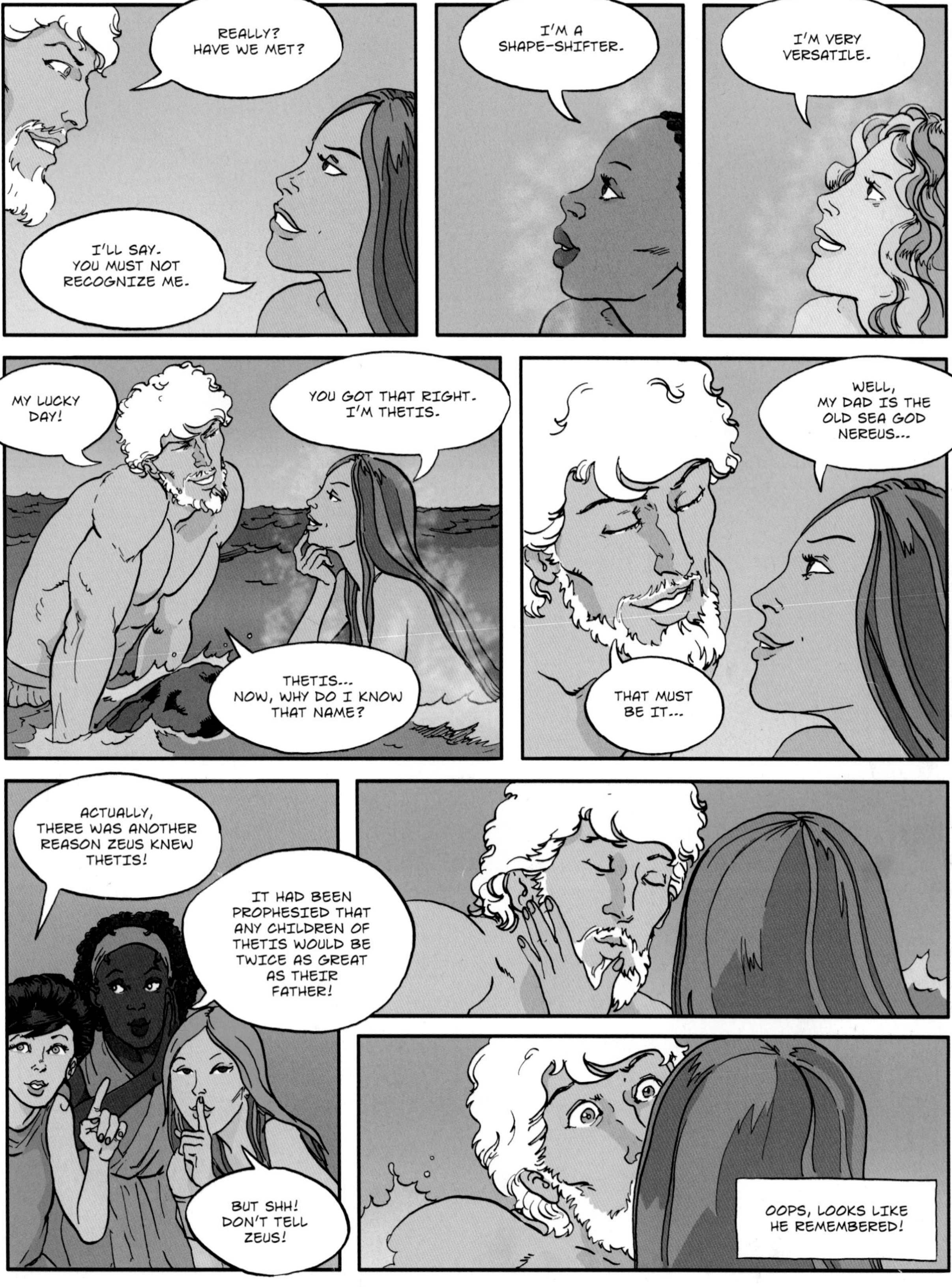
REALLY? HAVE WE MET?
I'LL SAY. YOU MUST NOT RECOGNIZE ME.
I'M A SHAPE-SHIFTER.
I'M VERY VERSATILE.
MY LUCKY DAY!
YOU GOT THAT RIGHT. I'M THETIS.
THETIS... NOW, WHY DO I KNOW THAT NAME?
WELL, MY DAD IS THE OLD SEA GOD NEREUS...
THAT MUST BE IT...
ACTUALLY, THERE WAS ANOTHER REASON ZEUS KNEW THETIS!
IT HAD BEEN PROPHESIED THAT ANY CHILDREN OF THETIS WOULD BE TWICE AS GREAT AS THEIR FATHER!
BUT SHH! DON'T TELL ZEUS!
OOPS, LOOKS LIKE HE REMEMBERED!

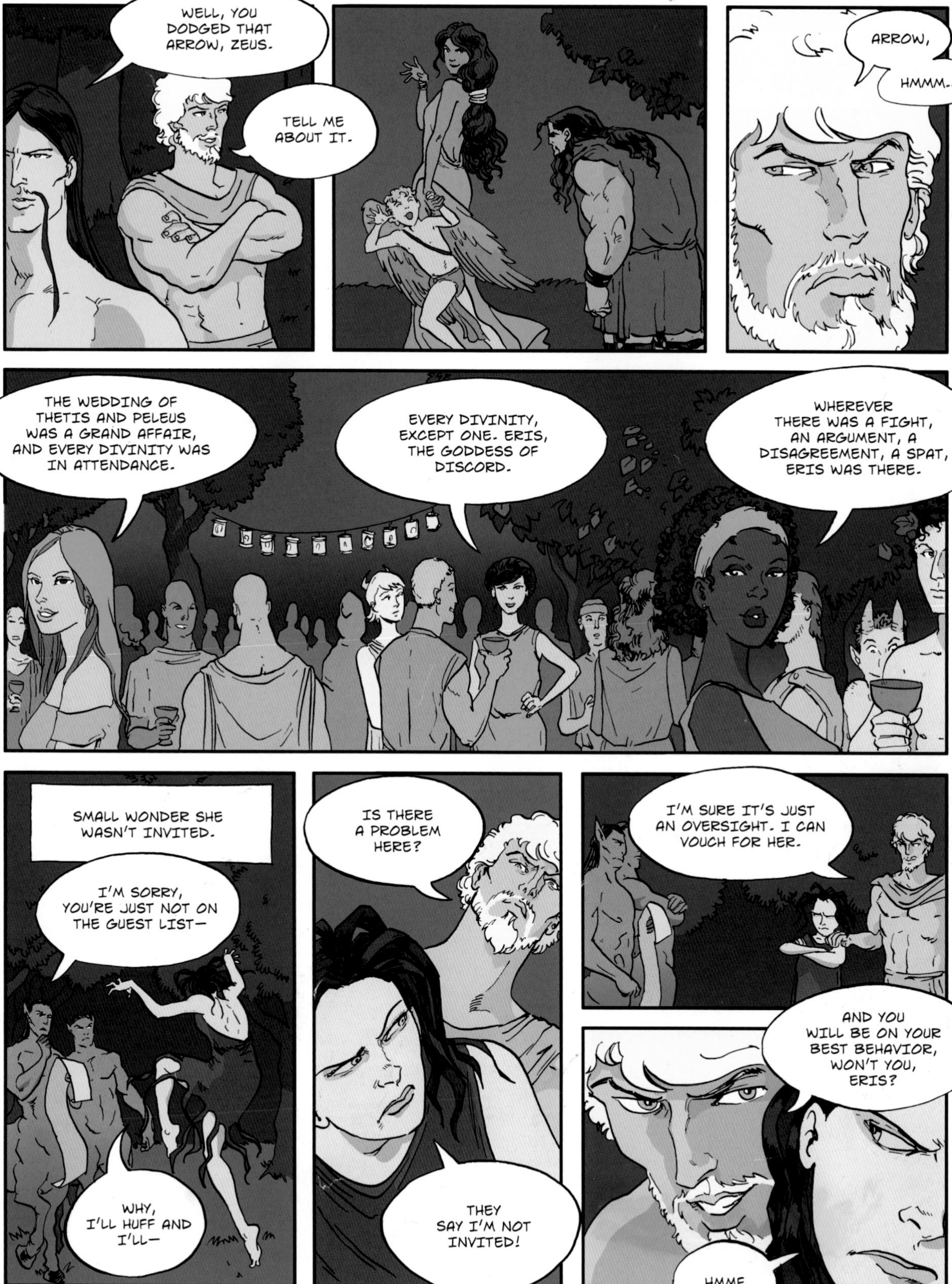
WELL, YOU DODGED THAT ARROW, ZEUS.
TELL ME ABOUT IT.
ARROW,
HMMM...
THE WEDDING OF THETIS AND PELEUS WAS A GRAND AFFAIR, AND EVERY DIVINITY WAS IN ATTENDANCE.
EVERY DIVINITY, EXCEPT ONE. ERIS, THE GODDESS OF DISCORD.
WHEREVER THERE WAS A FIGHT, AN ARGUMENT, A DISAGREEMENT, A SPAT, ERIS WAS THERE.
SMALL WONDER SHE WASN'T INVITED.
I'M SORRY, YOU'RE JUST NOT ON THE GUEST LIST—
WHY, I'LL HUFF AND I'LL—
IS THERE A PROBLEM HERE?
THEY SAY I'M NOT INVITED!
I'M SURE IT'S JUST AN OVERSIGHT. I CAN VOUCH FOR HER.
AND YOU WILL BE ON YOUR BEST BEHAVIOR, WON'T YOU, ERIS?
HMMF

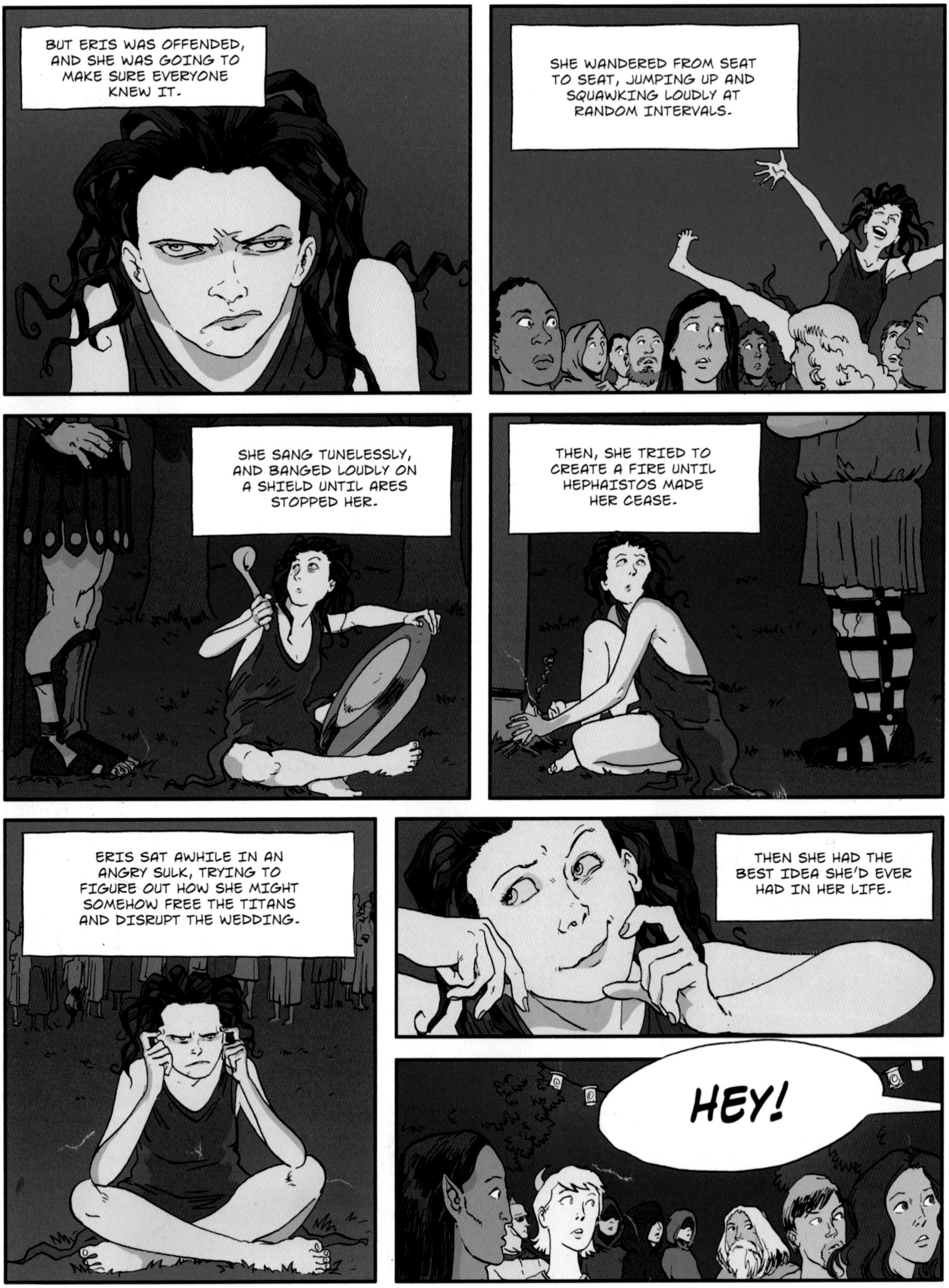
BUT ERIS WAS OFFENDED, AND SHE WAS GOING TO MAKE SURE EVERYONE KNEW IT.
SHE WANDERED FROM SEAT TO SEAT, JUMPING UP AND SQUAWKING LOUDLY AT RANDOM INTERVALS.
SHE SANG TUNELESSLY, AND BANGED LOUDLY ON A SHIELD UNTIL ARES STOPPED HER.
THEN, SHE TRIED TO CREATE A FIRE UNTIL HEPHAISTOS MADE HER CEASE.
ERIS SAT AWHILE IN AN ANGRY SULK, TRYING TO FIGURE OUT HOW SHE MIGHT SOMEHOW FREE THE TITANS AND DISRUPT THE WEDDING.
THEN SHE HAD THE BEST IDEA SHE'D EVER HAD IN HER LIFE.
HEY!

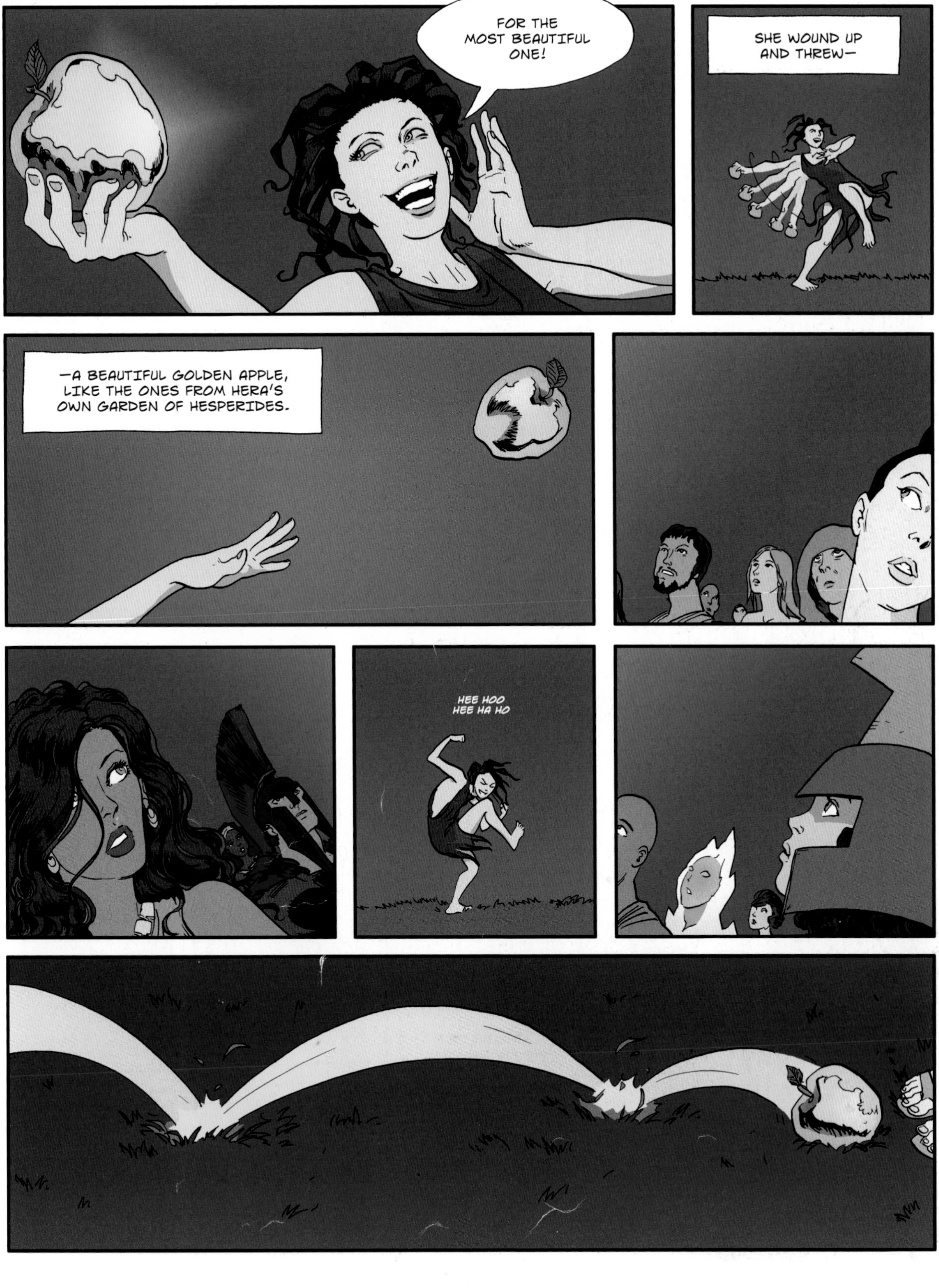
FOR THE MOST BEAUTIFUL ONE!
SHE WOUND UP AND THREW—
—A BEAUTIFUL GOLDEN APPLE, LIKE THE ONES FROM HERA'S OWN GARDEN OF HESPERIDES.
HEE HOO HEE HA HO

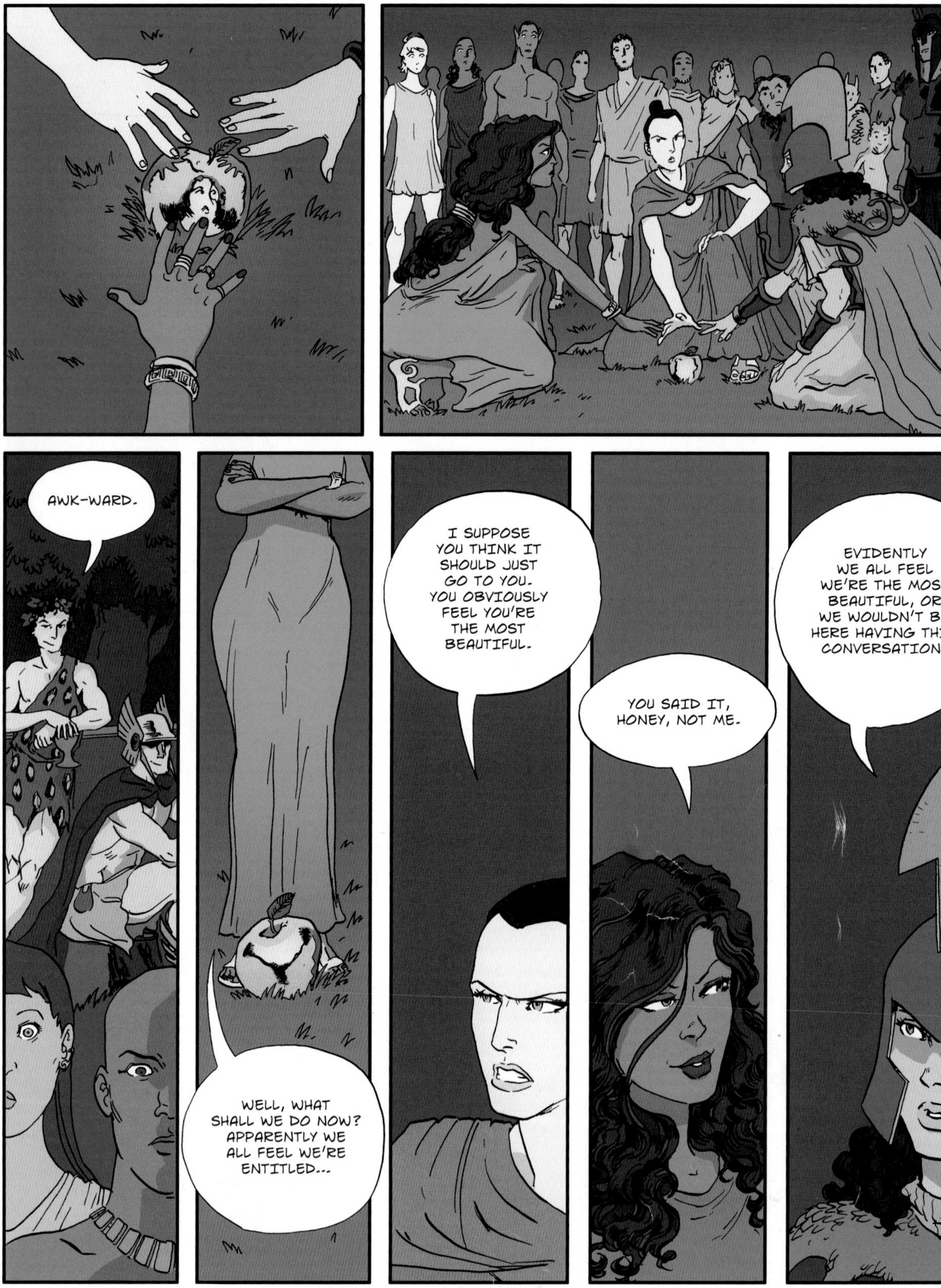
AWK-WARD.
WELL, WHAT SHALL WE DO NOW? APPARENTLY WE ALL FEEL WE'RE ENTITLED...
I SUPPOSE YOU THINK IT SHOULD JUST GO TO YOU. YOU OBVIOUSLY FEEL YOU'RE THE MOST BEAUTIFUL.
YOU SAID IT, HONEY, NOT ME.
EVIDENTLY WE ALL FEEL WE'RE THE MOST BEAUTIFUL, OR WE WOULDN'T BE HERE HAVING THIS CONVERSATION.

YEAH, AND ISN'T THAT A BIT OUT OF CHARACTER FOR YOU? SINCE WHEN DO YOU CARE ABOUT YOUR LOOKS?

I CARE VERY MUCH ABOUT MY APPEARANCE! JUST BECAUSE I DON'T DRESS LIKE A FLOOZY—

OH, A CUTTING REMARK FROM PALLAS ATHENA! I KNOW IT WAS DIRECTED AT ME BECAUSE I'M THE ONLY ONE HERE NOT DRESSED LIKE A SOLDIER OR A FRUMP!

WHAT IS THAT SUPPOSED TO MEAN? ARE YOU SAYING I DRESS UNFASHIONABLY?

IF THE SANDAL FITS, HERA.

MAYBE IF YOU CUT LOOSE EVERY ONCE IN A WHILE, YOUR HUSBAND—

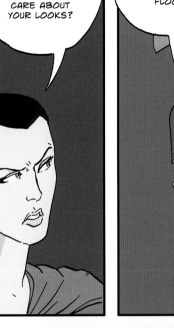

ZEUS!

WHAT'S GOING ON HERE?

WE NEED YOU TO SETTLE SOMETHING!

-PLE.

WHICHEVER ONE OF US IS THE MOST BEAUTIFUL GETS THIS AP—

THAT'S NOT YOURS.

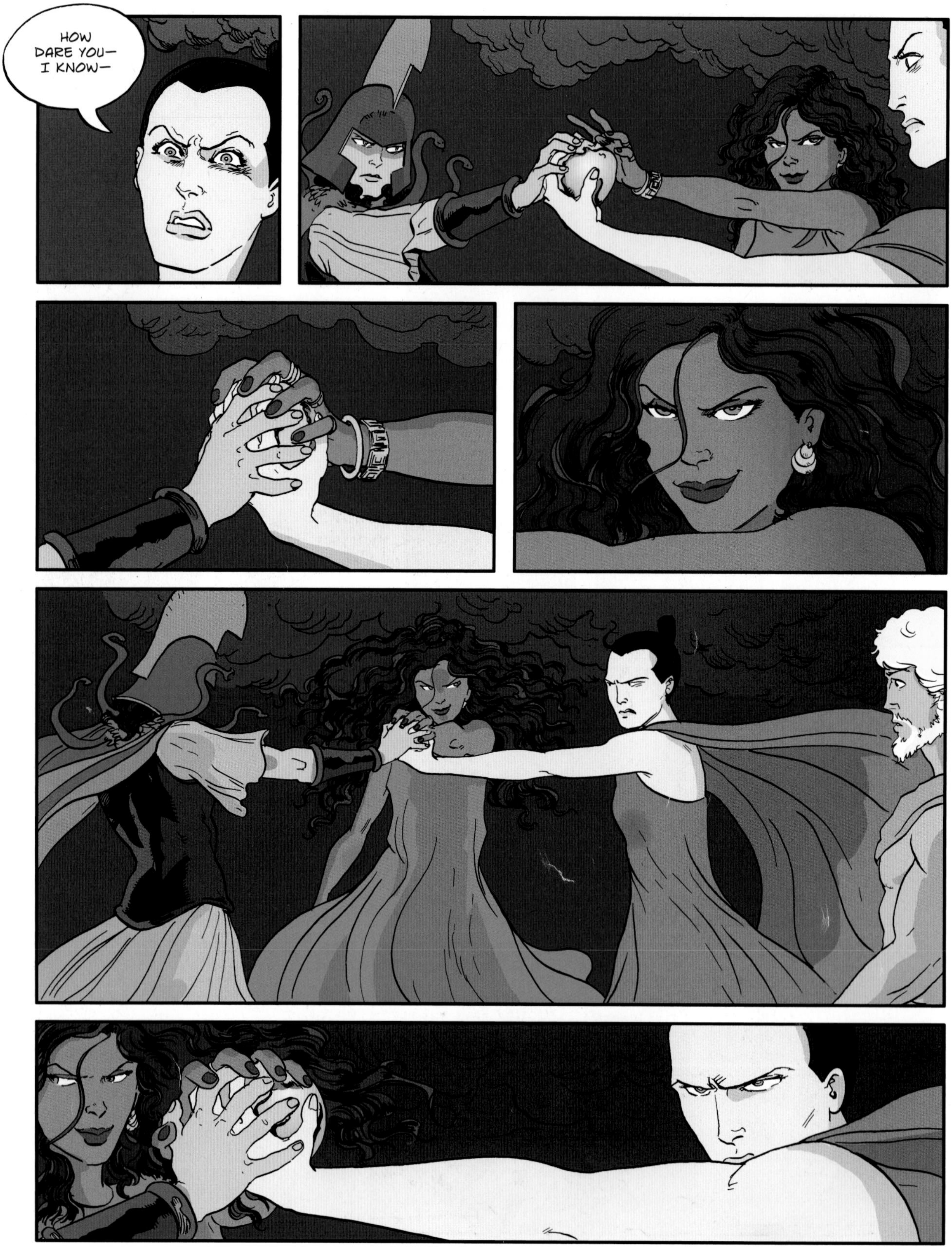
HOW DARE YOU— I KNOW—

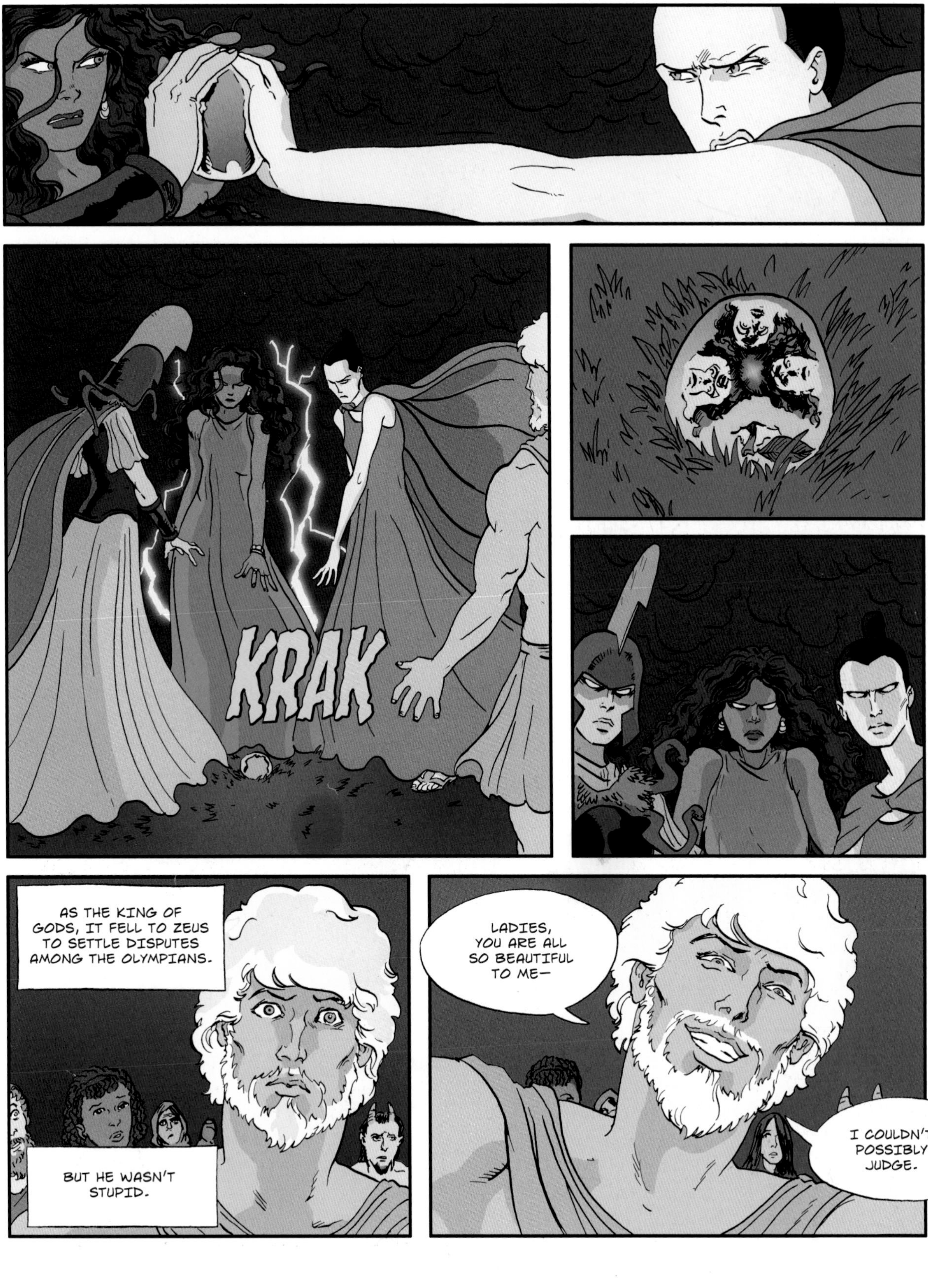
KRAK
AS THE KING OF GODS, IT FELL TO ZEUS TO SETTLE DISPUTES AMONG THE OLYMPIANS.
BUT HE WASN'T STUPID.
LADIES, YOU ARE ALL SO BEAUTIFUL TO ME—
I COULDN'T POSSIBLY JUDGE.

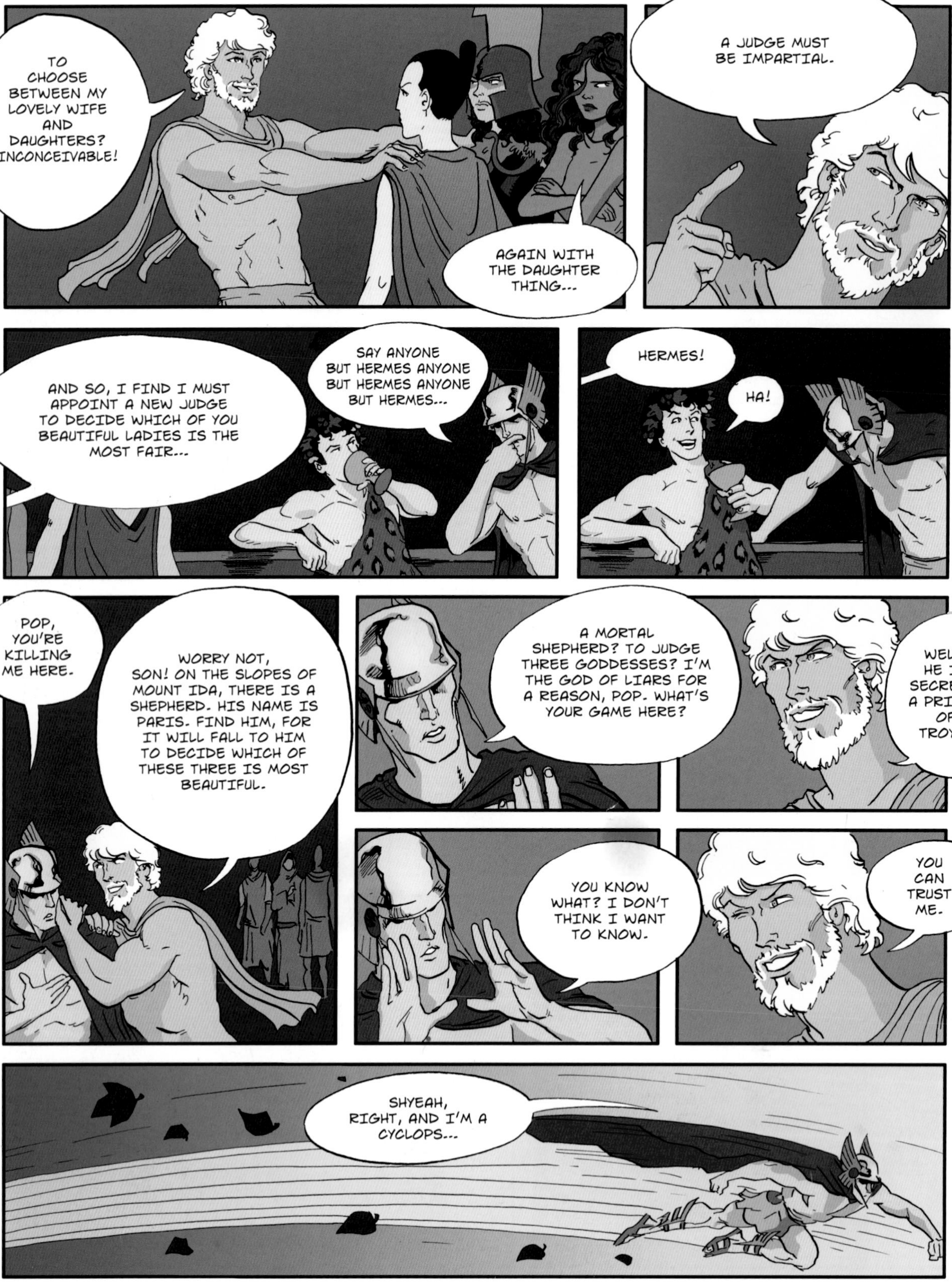
TO CHOOSE BETWEEN MY LOVELY WIFE AND DAUGHTERS? INCONCEIVABLE!
AGAIN WITH THE DAUGHTER THING...
A JUDGE MUST BE IMPARTIAL.
AND SO, I FIND I MUST APPOINT A NEW JUDGE TO DECIDE WHICH OF YOU BEAUTIFUL LADIES IS THE MOST FAIR...
SAY ANYONE BUT HERMES ANYONE BUT HERMES ANYONE BUT HERMES...
HERMES!
HA!
POP, YOU'RE KILLING ME HERE.
WORRY NOT, SON! ON THE SLOPES OF MOUNT IDA, THERE IS A SHEPHERD. HIS NAME IS PARIS. FIND HIM, FOR IT WILL FALL TO HIM TO DECIDE WHICH OF THESE THREE IS MOST BEAUTIFUL.
A MORTAL SHEPHERD? TO JUDGE THREE GODDESSES? I'M THE GOD OF LIARS FOR A REASON, POP. WHAT'S YOUR GAME HERE?
WELL, HE IS SECRETLY A PRINCE OF TROY...
YOU KNOW WHAT? I DON'T THINK I WANT TO KNOW.
YOU CAN TRUST ME.
SHYEAH, RIGHT, AND I'M A CYCLOPS...

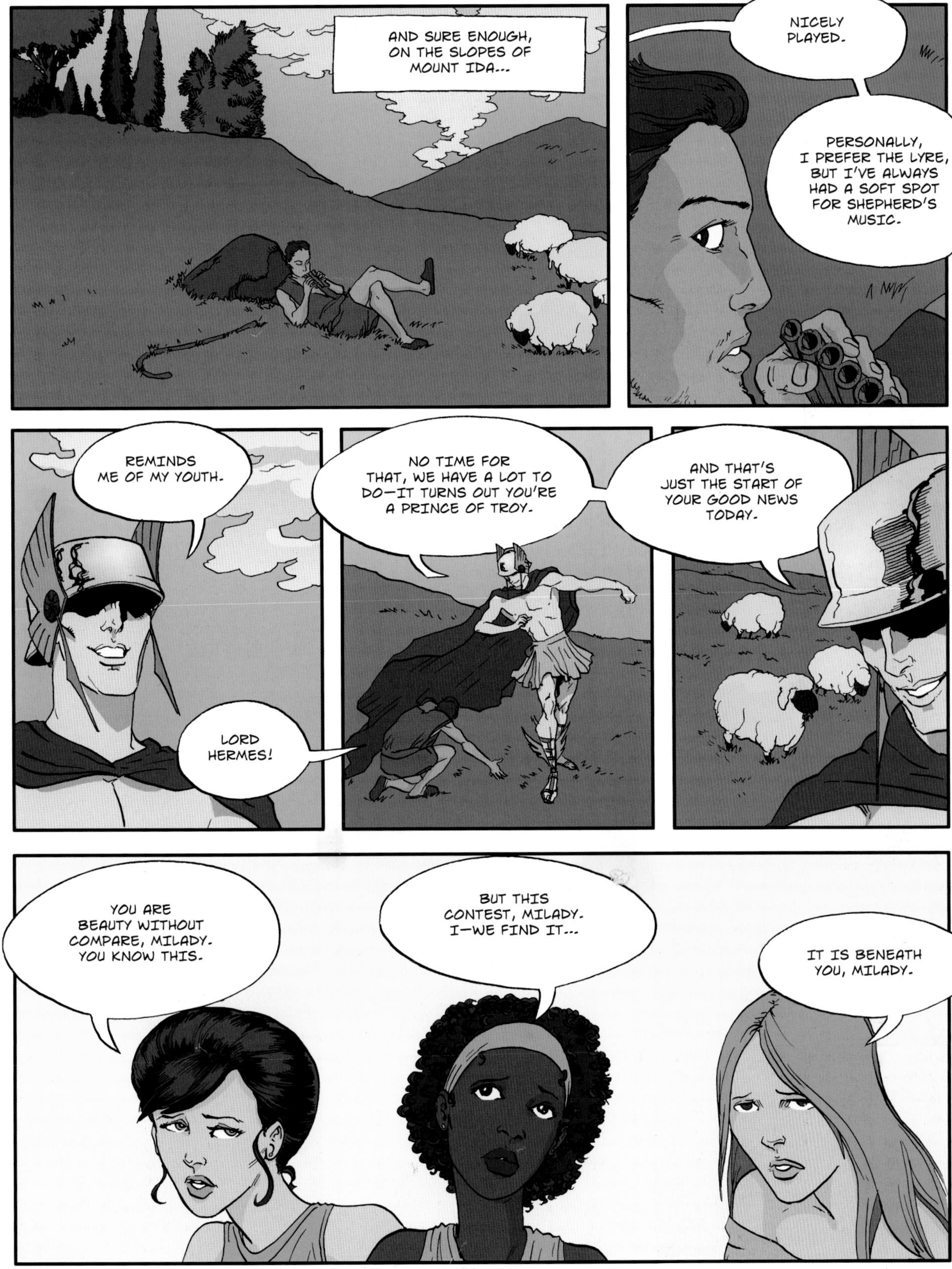
AND SURE ENOUGH, ON THE SLOPES OF MOUNT IDA...
NICELY PLAYED.
PERSONALLY, I PREFER THE LYRE, BUT I'VE ALWAYS HAD A SOFT SPOT FOR SHEPHERD'S MUSIC.
REMINDS ME OF MY YOUTH.
LORD HERMES!
NO TIME FOR THAT, WE HAVE A LOT TO DO—IT TURNS OUT YOU'RE A PRINCE OF TROY.
AND THAT'S JUST THE START OF YOUR GOOD NEWS TODAY.
YOU ARE BEAUTY WITHOUT COMPARE, MILADY. YOU KNOW THIS.
BUT THIS CONTEST, MILADY. I—WE FIND IT...
IT IS BENEATH YOU, MILADY.

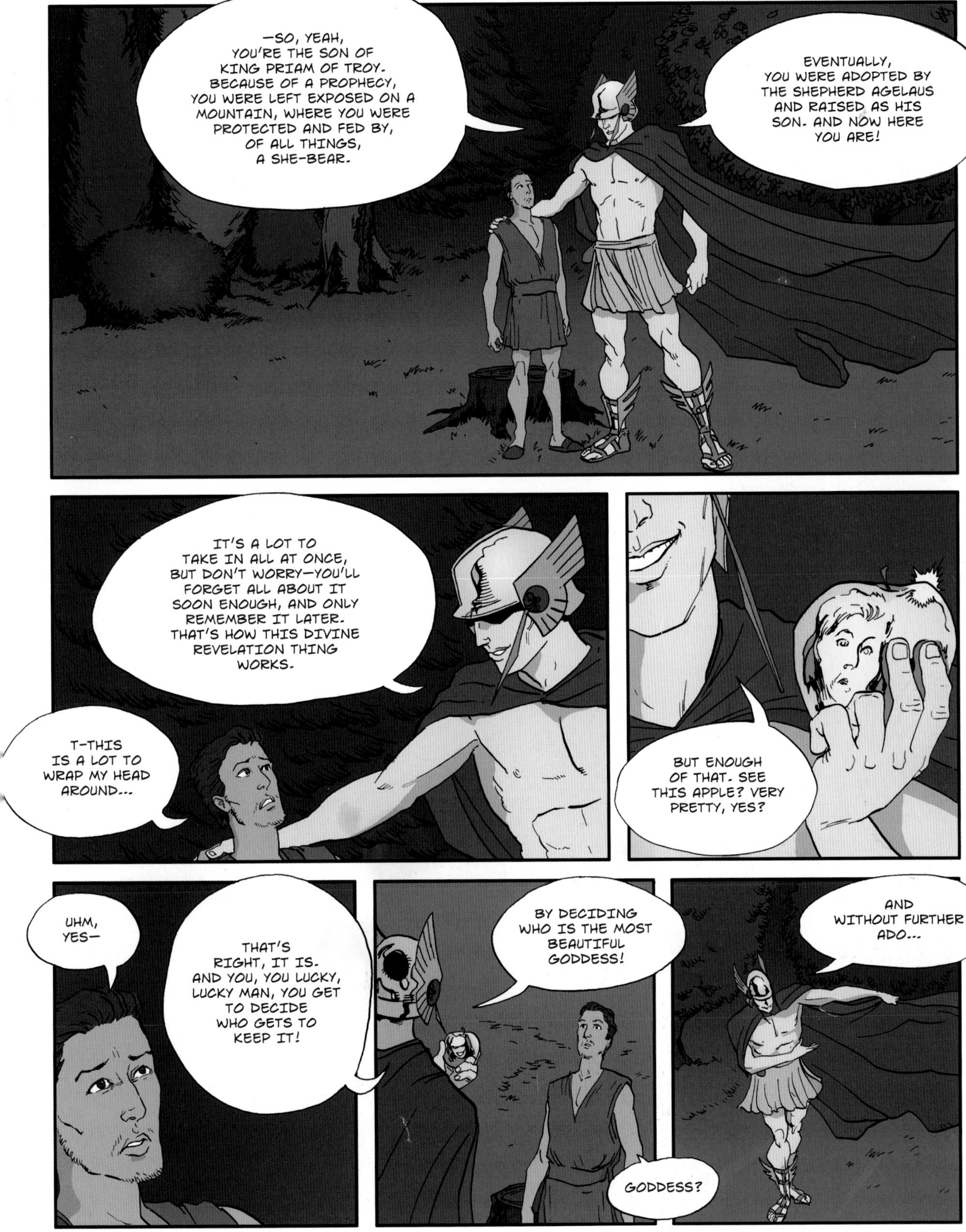
—SO, YEAH, YOU'RE THE SON OF KING PRIAM OF TROY. BECAUSE OF A PROPHECY, YOU WERE LEFT EXPOSED ON A MOUNTAIN, WHERE YOU WERE PROTECTED AND FED BY, OF ALL THINGS, A SHE-BEAR.
EVENTUALLY, YOU WERE ADOPTED BY THE SHEPHERD AGELAUS AND RAISED AS HIS SON. AND NOW HERE YOU ARE!
IT'S A LOT TO TAKE IN ALL AT ONCE, BUT DON'T WORRY—YOU'LL FORGET ALL ABOUT IT SOON ENOUGH, AND ONLY REMEMBER IT LATER. THAT'S HOW THIS DIVINE REVELATION THING WORKS.
T-THIS IS A LOT TO WRAP MY HEAD AROUND...
BUT ENOUGH OF THAT. SEE THIS APPLE? VERY PRETTY, YES?
UHM, YES—
THAT'S RIGHT, IT IS. AND YOU, YOU LUCKY, LUCKY MAN, YOU GET TO DECIDE WHO GETS TO KEEP IT!
BY DECIDING WHO IS THE MOST BEAUTIFUL GODDESS!
GODDESS?
AND WITHOUT FURTHER ADO...

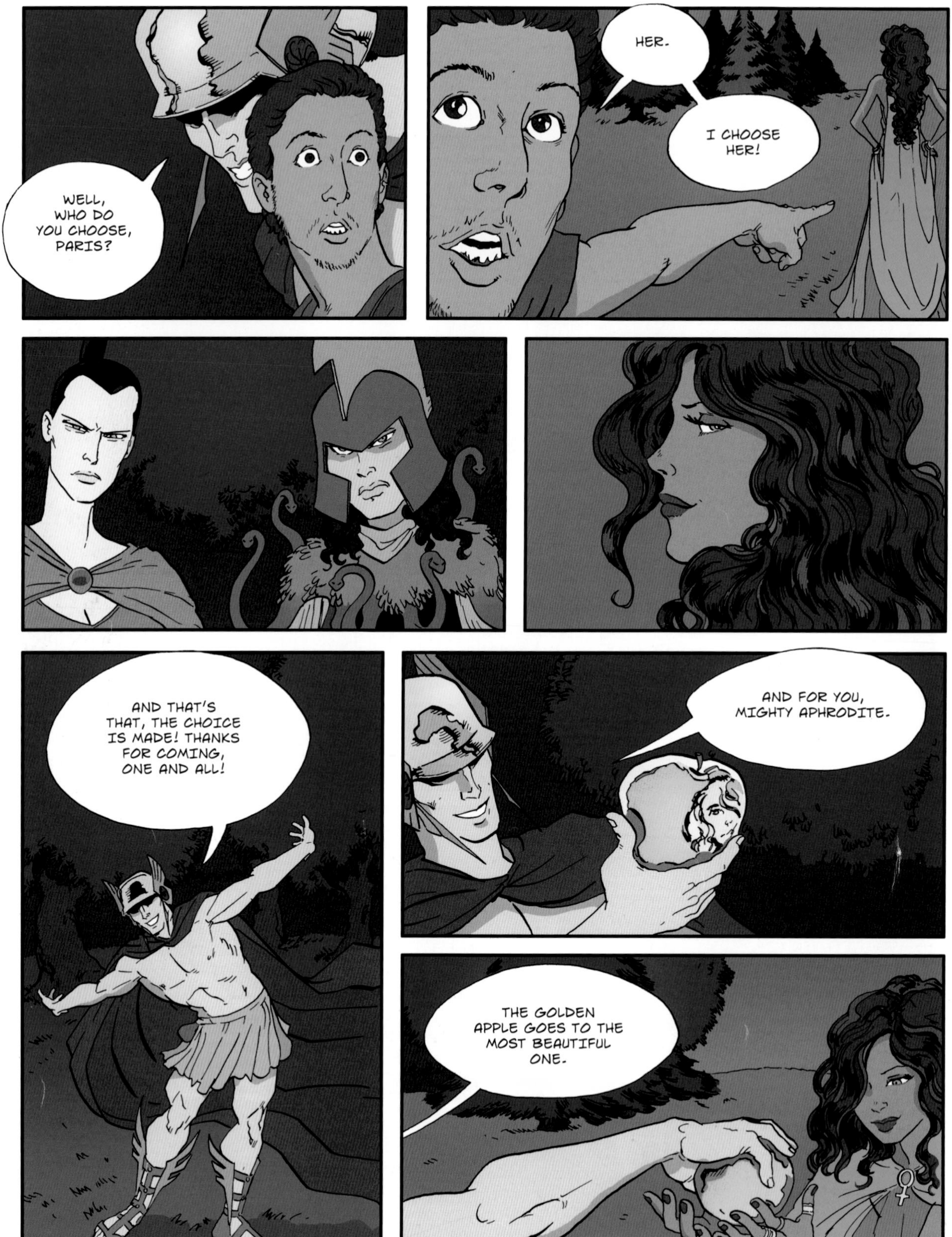
WELL, WHO DO YOU CHOOSE, PARIS?
HER.
I CHOOSE HER!
AND THAT'S THAT, THE CHOICE IS MADE! THANKS FOR COMING, ONE AND ALL!
AND FOR YOU, MIGHTY APHRODITE.
THE GOLDEN APPLE GOES TO THE MOST BEAUTIFUL ONE.

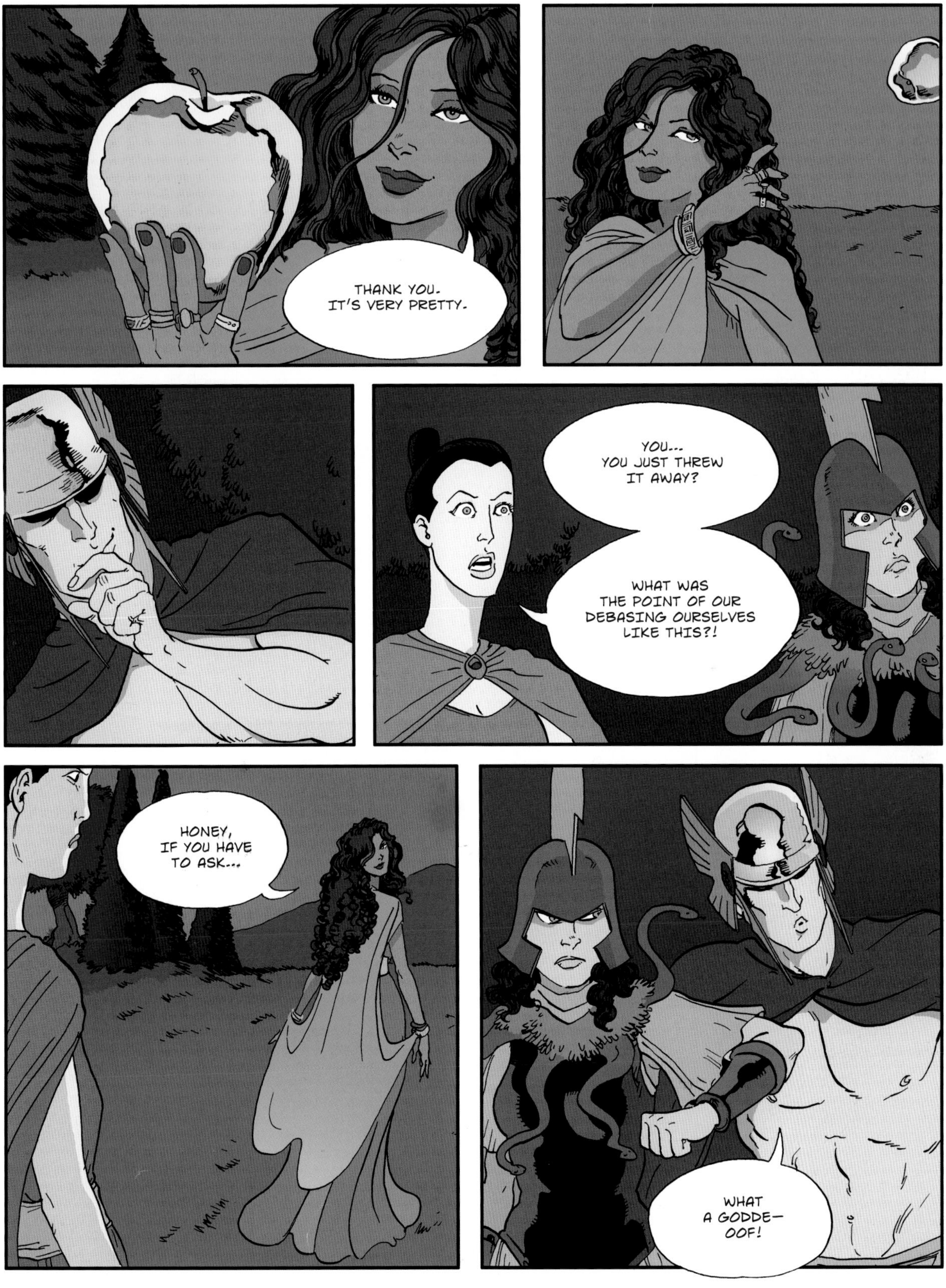
THANK YOU. IT'S VERY PRETTY.
YOU... YOU JUST THREW IT AWAY?
WHAT WAS THE POINT OF OUR DEBASING OURSELVES LIKE THIS?!
HONEY, IF YOU HAVE TO ASK...
WHAT A GODDE— OOF!

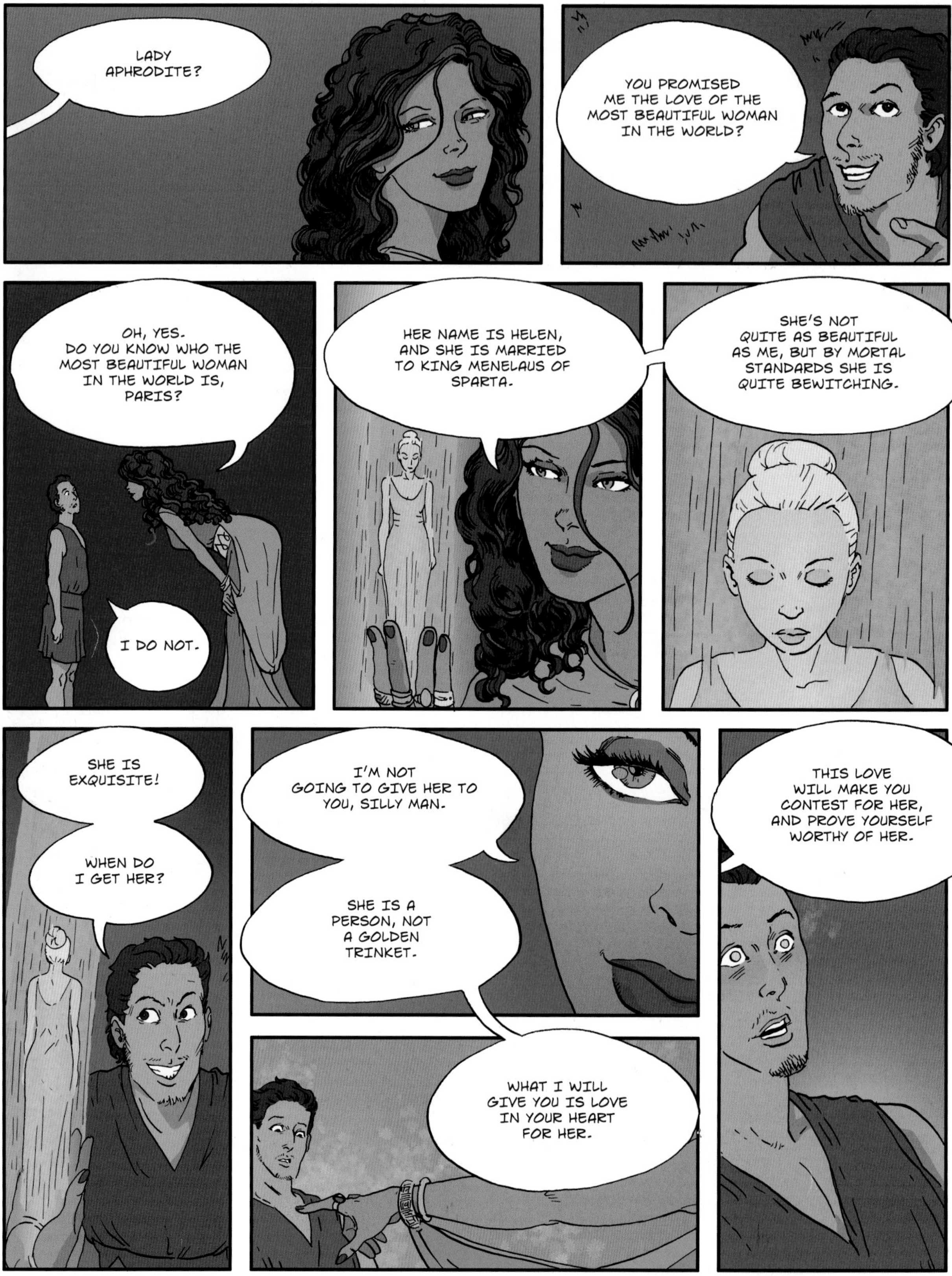
LADY APHRODITE?
YOU PROMISED ME THE LOVE OF THE MOST BEAUTIFUL WOMAN IN THE WORLD?
OH, YES. DO YOU KNOW WHO THE MOST BEAUTIFUL WOMAN IN THE WORLD IS, PARIS?
I DO NOT.
HER NAME IS HELEN, AND SHE IS MARRIED TO KING MENELAUS OF SPARTA.
SHE'S NOT QUITE AS BEAUTIFUL AS ME, BUT BY MORTAL STANDARDS SHE IS QUITE BEWITCHING.
SHE IS EXQUISITE!
WHEN DO I GET HER?
I'M NOT GOING TO GIVE HER TO YOU, SILLY MAN.
SHE IS A PERSON, NOT A GOLDEN TRINKET.
WHAT I WILL GIVE YOU IS LOVE IN YOUR HEART FOR HER.
THIS LOVE WILL MAKE YOU CONTEST FOR HER, AND PROVE YOURSELF WORTHY OF HER.

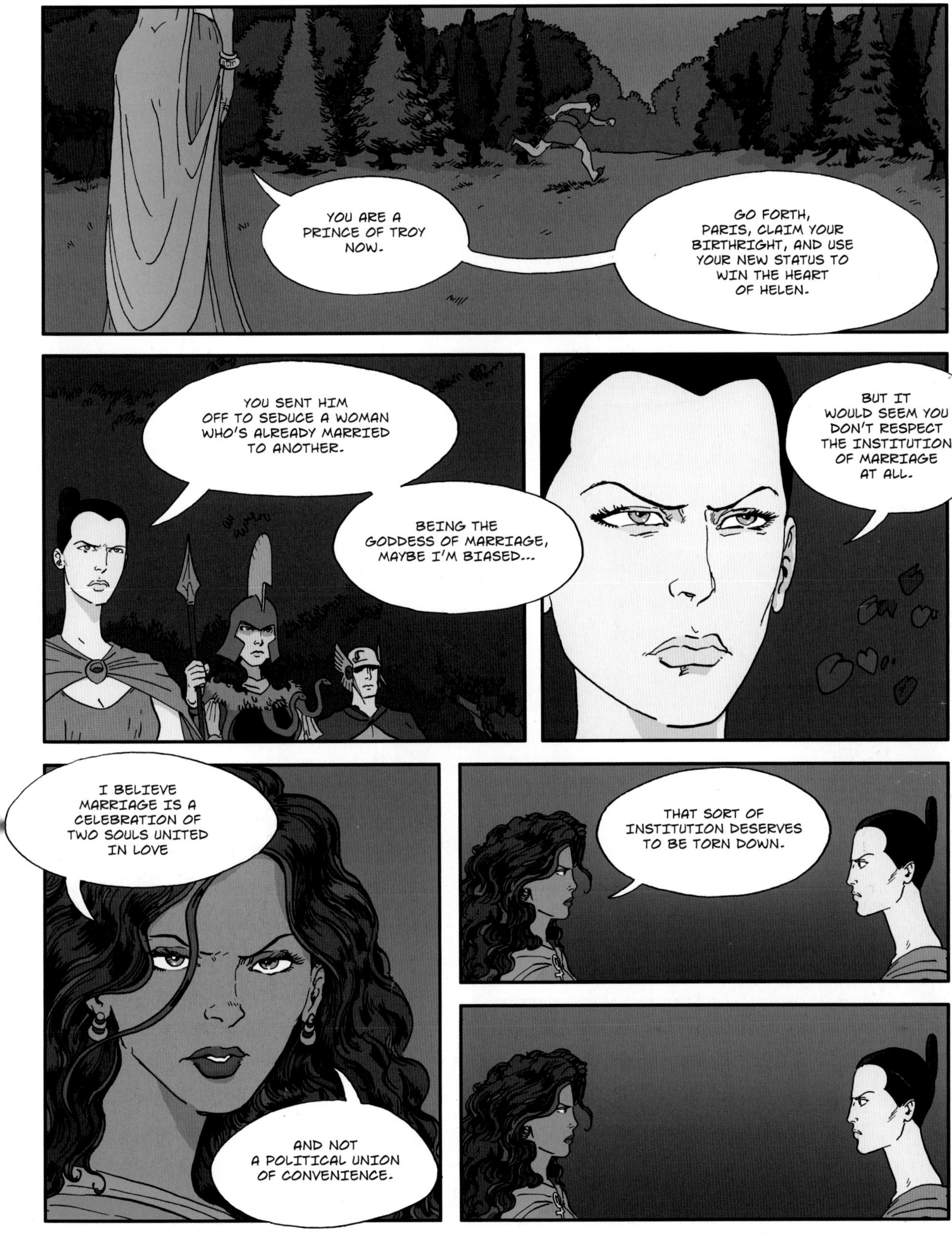
YOU ARE A PRINCE OF TROY NOW.
GO FORTH, PARIS, CLAIM YOUR BIRTHRIGHT, AND USE YOUR NEW STATUS TO WIN THE HEART OF HELEN.
YOU SENT HIM OFF TO SEDUCE A WOMAN WHO'S ALREADY MARRIED TO ANOTHER.
BEING THE GODDESS OF MARRIAGE, MAYBE I'M BIASED...
BUT IT WOULD SEEM YOU DON'T RESPECT THE INSTITUTION OF MARRIAGE AT ALL.
I BELIEVE MARRIAGE IS A CELEBRATION OF TWO SOULS UNITED IN LOVE
AND NOT A POLITICAL UNION OF CONVENIENCE.
THAT SORT OF INSTITUTION DESERVES TO BE TORN DOWN.

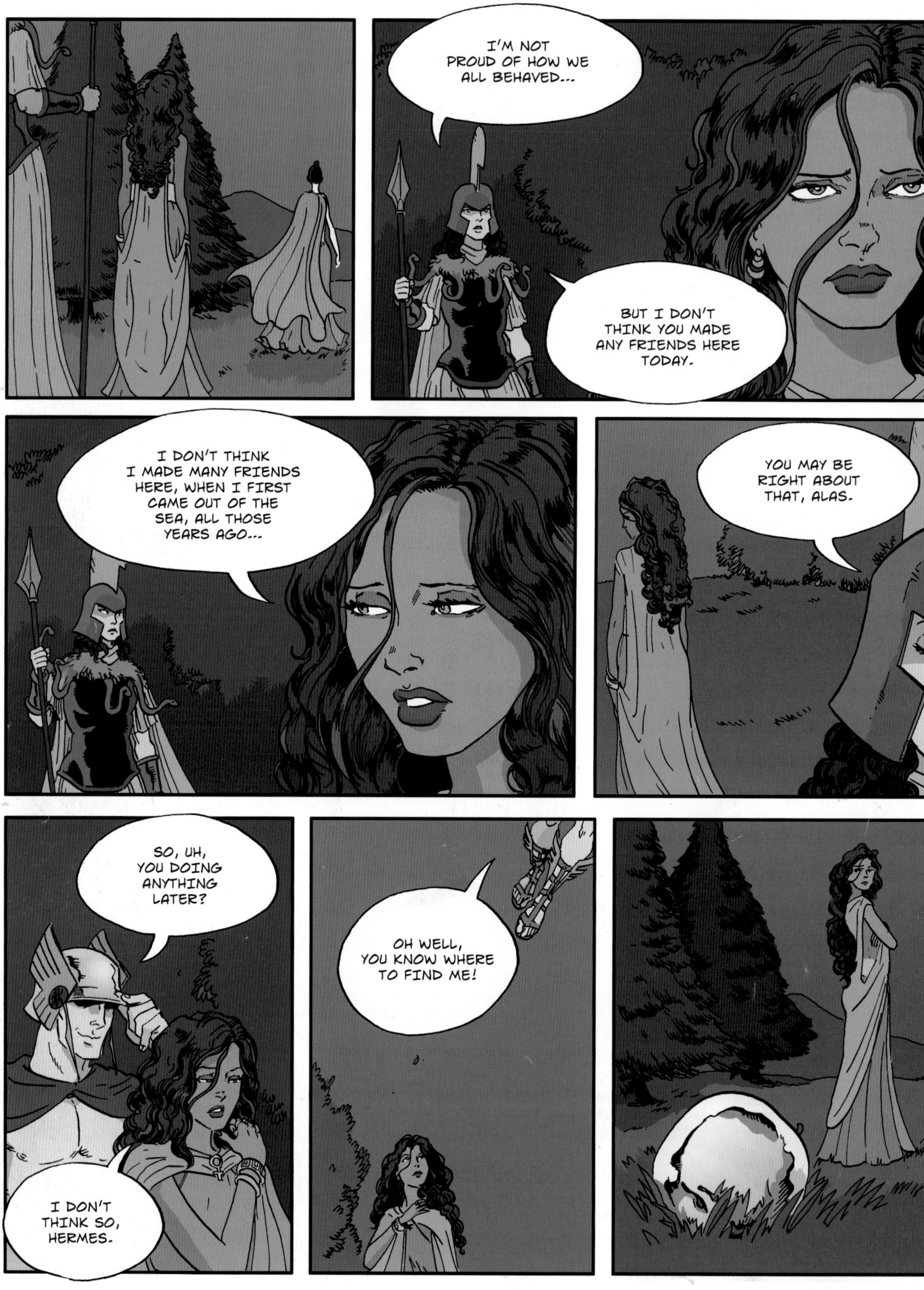
I'M NOT PROUD OF HOW WE ALL BEHAVED...
BUT I DON'T THINK YOU MADE ANY FRIENDS HERE TODAY.
I DON'T THINK I MADE MANY FRIENDS HERE, WHEN I FIRST CAME OUT OF THE SEA, ALL THOSE YEARS AGO...
YOU MAY BE RIGHT ABOUT THAT, ALAS.
SO, UH, YOU DOING ANYTHING LATER?
I DON'T THINK SO, HERMES.
OH WELL, YOU KNOW WHERE TO FIND ME!

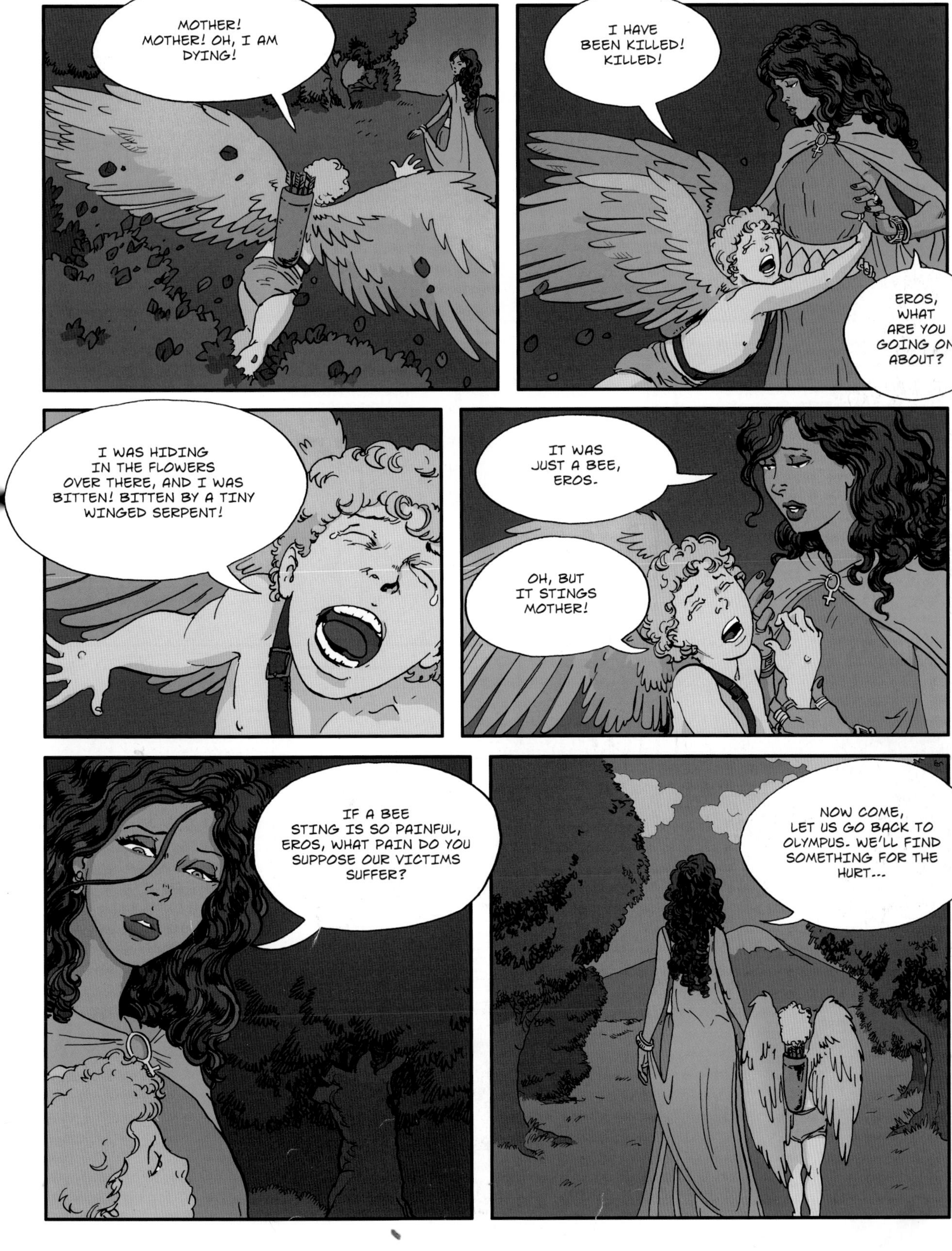
MOTHER! MOTHER! OH, I AM DYING!
I HAVE BEEN KILLED! KILLED!
EROS, WHAT ARE YOU GOING ON ABOUT?
I WAS HIDING IN THE FLOWERS OVER THERE, AND I WAS BITTEN! BITTEN BY A TINY WINGED SERPENT!
IT WAS JUST A BEE, EROS.
OH, BUT IT STINGS MOTHER!
IF A BEE STING IS SO PAINFUL, EROS, WHAT PAIN DO YOU SUPPOSE OUR VICTIMS SUFFER?
NOW COME, LET US GO BACK TO OLYMPUS. WE'LL FIND SOMETHING FOR THE HURT...

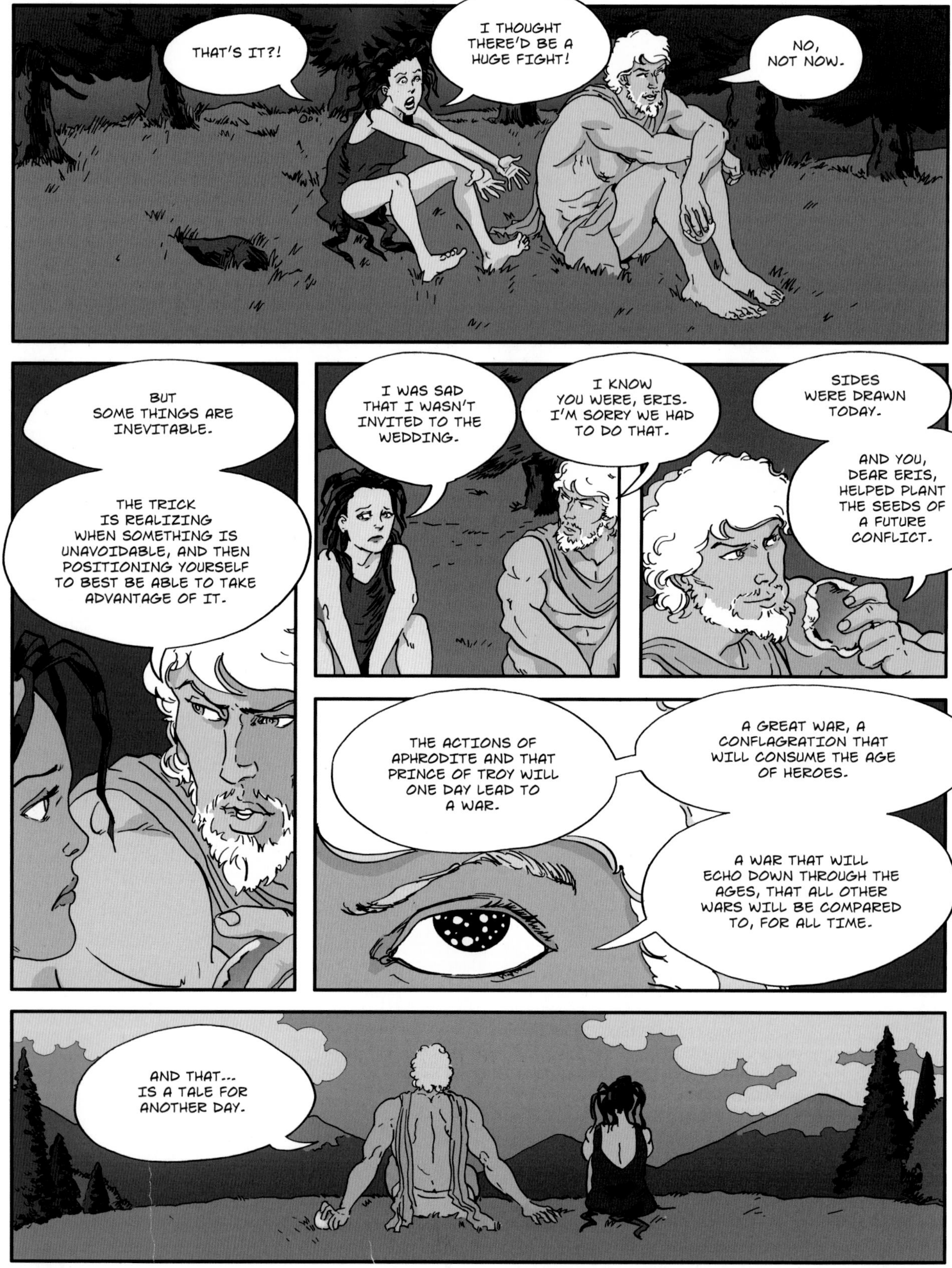
THAT'S IT?!
I THOUGHT THERE'D BE A HUGE FIGHT!
NO, NOT NOW.
BUT SOME THINGS ARE INEVITABLE.
THE TRICK IS REALIZING WHEN SOMETHING IS UNAVOIDABLE, AND THEN POSITIONING YOURSELF TO BEST BE ABLE TO TAKE ADVANTAGE OF IT.
I WAS SAD THAT I WASN'T INVITED TO THE WEDDING.
I KNOW YOU WERE, ERIS. I'M SORRY WE HAD TO DO THAT.
SIDES WERE DRAWN TODAY.
AND YOU, DEAR ERIS, HELPED PLANT THE SEEDS OF A FUTURE CONFLICT.
THE ACTIONS OF APHRODITE AND THAT PRINCE OF TROY WILL ONE DAY LEAD TO A WAR.
A GREAT WAR, A CONFLAGRATION THAT WILL CONSUME THE AGE OF HEROES.
A WAR THAT WILL ECHO DOWN THROUGH THE AGES, THAT ALL OTHER WARS WILL BE COMPARED TO, FOR ALL TIME.
AND THAT... IS A TALE FOR ANOTHER DAY.

AUTHOR'S NOTE

Of all the gods and goddesses I have drawn for OLYMPIANS, it took me the longest time to nail down the look of Aphrodite. In fact, if you look at her cameo appearance on the last page of OLYMPIANS Book 1, *Zeus: King of the Gods*, she's not quite there yet—she's more of a proto-Aphrodite. She doesn't really arrive in her present guise until the third volume of the series, *Hera: The Goddess and Her Glory*. I suppose this late development is appropriate for a goddess who, as we saw in this book, spent so much time developing herself.

Let me cut myself a break, though: designing a visage for the most beautiful goddess of Olympus is a pretty difficult and daunting task. All of the Olympians are meant to be beautiful (except poor Hephaistos). How to distinguish the goddess of beauty from a family filled with beautiful goddesses? It makes one appreciate how difficult it must have been for Paris to make his choice among them in the contest for Eris's golden apple.

The Judgment of Paris, a major component of this book you're reading right now, was difficult to realize for another reason—it doesn't really reflect that well on the three contestants. Athena, Hera, and Aphrodite are the three most powerful goddesses on Olympus, and they get involved in a petty squabble over who's prettiest? It seems to me to be out of

character for all the parties involved. Does warrior goddess Athena *really* care about how she looks? Does Hera, who has a golden apple tree in her Garden of Hesperides, *really* need another one? Does Aphrodite, the goddess of beauty, *really* need justification for her looks from a mortal prince? Frankly, it all feels a bit sexist.

Let's keep in mind that it's Zeus who originally set this whole thing in motion. Zeus, from the moment he first met Aphrodite as she walked from the sea, sized her up and realized: this woman can cause trouble for me. The same is true of Hera, his wife, the only being he truly fears. And also of Athena, the daughter who had been fated to overthrow him. These were some very, very powerful women, and Zeus was afraid of their power. And so, in my

As almost always happens with OLYMPIANS, I finished this book with a much greater understanding of and affinity for its subject, Aphrodite. As the goddess of love and attraction, her power holds sway over everything that lives, even Zeus. I would argue that makes her, in her own way, the most powerful god on Olympus, and more than deserving of her win in the Judgment of Paris. I can't say that if I were in Paris's shoes I would have given her the apple (there's some pretty cool stuff in Asia), but I can certainly respect Aphrodite and her power.

George O'Connor
Brooklyn, NY
2013

retelling of this tale, I decided it wasn't *really* about who was the most beautiful goddess. It was a power struggle.

Olympus might be the tallest mountain left standing after the clash of Gods and Titans (I sneak that line in every volume of OLYMPIANS), but it's only so big—maybe not big enough for three goddesses of such power as Aphrodite, Athena, and Hera, especially given their widely varying temperaments. I think that's reflected even in the ancient retellings of this myth. It's always about the various prizes that the goddesses offer Paris, not about how they look, not really.

APHRODITE
THE MOST BEAUTIFUL GODDESS

GODDESS OF   Beauty and Love

ROMAN NAME   . . . and Venus was her name

SYMBOLS   Mirror, Seashell

SACRED ANIMALS   Dove, Sparrow, Fish

SACRED PLANTS   Rose, Anemone, Myrtle

SACRED PLACES   Cyprus (thought to be the first island she set foot on), Cythera (in contention with Cyprus as the first island Aphrodite set foot on)

DAY OF THE WEEK   Friday

MONTH   April

HEAVENLY BODY   The planet Venus

MODERN LEGACY   A love potion is still known as an aphrodisiac, after Aphrodite.

♀, the gender symbol for women, is a representation of Aphrodite's mirror.

Many more references to Aphrodite can be found under her Roman name, Venus, such as both the Venus flytrap and the professional tennis player Venus Williams.

G^REEK NOTES

PAGE 1: Hmm, this seems familiar . . . Longtime readers of OLYMPIANS will note that this page and the following sequence mirror the opening of *Zeus: King of the Gods*. Think of this as the behind-the-scenes version.

PAGE 2, PANEL 1: True story: I originally wanted to call this book *Aphrodite: The Power of Love*, until my editor said it reminded him of the song "Power of Love" by Huey Lewis and the News. If you don't know who that is, I'll wait here while you go look it up on YouTube. No offense to Mr. Lewis or his Newshounds, but that certainly ruined that title for me.

PAGE 6, PANEL 3: If you have a copy handy, go look at page 8, panel 5 of *Zeus: King of the Gods*—"What came from that is a tale for another day." Today's that day.

PAGE 6, PANEL 5: Offspring of the Titans—that's Eos, the rosy-fingered dawn.

PAGE 6, PANEL 6: Helios, the sun, rising above the Oceanides frolicking in the sea.

PAGE 6, PANEL 7: Some second-generation Titans, notably Atlas, Prometheus, and Epimetheus.

PAGE 6, PANEL 8: And finally, Selene, the moon.

PAGE 8, PANEL 1: Left to right: Hestia, Hades, Hera, Zeus, Poseidon, Demeter, and Metis.

PAGE 8, PANEL 2: Left to right: Ares, Hephaistos, Athena, Apollo, Artemis, and Kore (later renamed Persephone).

PAGE 8, PANELS 3-6: The animals pictured here are all representative in some way of Aphrodite and her power. The clown fish in panel 6 are no doubt looking for Nemo.

PAGE 9: This bit about the foam creating a mind for itself, and creating a self-perfected form is an interesting bit of imagery I got from the *Dionysiaca*, by the Egyptian-Greek writer Nonnus.

PAGE 11, PANEL 1: I know that for the longest time I had a problem understanding why Zephyros, the West Wind, was the wind that first discovered Aphrodite, who came out of the East. To clear up any potential confusion, the West Wind blows from the West, in an eastward direction. Now that's not confusing at all, is it?

PAGE 14, PANEL 3: I like to think this is what inspired the events of OLYMPIANS Book 4, *Hades: Lord of the Dead*.

PAGE 15, PANEL 1: That's because Zeus really likes the ladies.

PAGE 16: Fun fact: When I originally laid out and scripted this page, the part of Apollo was played by Hermes, and the part of Ares was played by Apollo. Then I realized that at the time of Aphrodite's ascension, Hermes wouldn't have been born yet (he's the second youngest Olympian).

PAGE 19, PANELS 6-9: This prefigures one of the most famous affairs in Greek mythology, that between Ares and Aphrodite.

PAGE 20, PANEL 3: Hestia, Athena, and Artemis were the maiden goddesses and as such were (largely) outside of the reach of Aphrodite's power. I bet that bugged her.

PAGE 21: Again, Zeus really likes the ladies.

PAGE 22, PANEL 2: Most ancient sources agree that Aphrodite was born from the sea foam (her name even contains the Greek word for foam, *aphros*), but no less a source than Homer himself names her as a daughter of Zeus and Dione, one of the Oceanides. I included this scene as a nod to the notion of Zeus as her father, especially since, as Athena points out, it's quite out of character for him not to join in with the other gods in trying to crush on Aphrodite. I may have mentioned this before, but Zeus likes the ladies.

PAGE 22, PANEL 6: Nectar and ambrosia are the drink and food of the gods on Olympus.

PAGE 23 PANEL 2: Hephaistos was widely believed to have suffered from a disability in his legs—he was famously referred to as walking crooked, like a flickering flame. That's why he's late to the party, and why the trail behind him is so jagged.

PAGE 24, PANEL 1: Hephaistos's great-uncles, the Cyclopes, worked with him in his forge in Mount Aetna in Sicily.

PAGE 29: Here's a breakdown of the myths shown in cameo on this page

PANEL 1: These are the Kerastai, horned humans who lived on Aphrodite's beloved Cyprus. They hung out around a temple/shelter dedicated to Zeus and brutally murdered the guests. This angered the goddess of love, and she turned them into bulls.

PANEL 2: Boutes was one of the Argonauts (last seen in OLYMPIANS Book 3, *Hera: The Goddess and Her Glory*). He was rescued by Aphrodite from the seducing song of the Sirens (last seen in OLYMPIANS Book 4, *Hades: Lord of the Dead*).

PANEL 3: This is Adonis, a famous mortal fling of Aphrodite. He was famous for being beautiful, and you'll still hear his name evoked today to describe a particularly handsome fella. On the right of the panel is a jealous Ares, in the form of a boar. He's totally about to kill Adonis.

PANEL 4: Here's another very, very attractive man, Narcissus. A bunch of nymphs had crushes on him, but he had eyes only for himself. They prayed to Aphrodite, who arranged that he literally fell in love with his reflection. He stared so long as his reflection that he finally turned into a flower, named, of course, the narcissus. A person who is too self-absorbed is still called a narcissist.

PAGE 35, PANEL 3: I based the statue that Aphrodite is referring to on the *Aphrodite of Knidos*, created by the famed Greek sculptor Praxiteles.

PAGE 37, PANEL 3: Not to be confused with the nymph Galatea from page 17 of OLYMPIANS, Book 5, *Poseidon:*

Earth Shaker. Interestingly, the ivory statue is never named in any ancient sources; she only acquired the name Galatea in (relatively) modern times. I normally use only classical sources for OLYMPIANS, but in this instance, I felt the poor statue deserved a name, for goodness' sake. Appropriately for an ivory statue, Galatea means "milky white."

PAGE 40: Judging from this page, it might be surmised that Eros is a little bit of a punk.

PAGE 43: Remember on page 56 of OLYMPIANS Book 5, *Poseidon: Earth Shaker,* when an unseen girlfriend of Zeus summons Briareos, one of the Hekatonchieres, to free Zeus from his bondage? That was Thetis, seen here.

PAGE 44, PANEL 1: Thetis later gives birth to the great Greek hero Achilles, protagonist of the *Iliad*. A nigh invulnerable warrior, he certainly is far greater than his father, but nowhere near a god.

PAGE 46: This whole sequence, in which Eris acts up at the wedding of Thetis, comes from the account by Colluthus. All of her actions are so bizarre that I just had to include it.

PAGE 47, PANEL 3: The Greeks really loved golden apples.

PAGE 52, PANEL 6: Zeus is really playing a long con here. He's tricksy like that. Incidentally, in case you were wondering, there is no connection between Paris the mythological figure and Paris the city. *Quelle coincidence!*

PAGE 53, PANEL 2: I'm trying to be clever here. Hermes prefers the lyre because he invented it as a child. His soft spot for shepherd's music is owing to his origins as a rustic god of shepherds before expanding into his later role as the busiest deity on Olympus.

PAGE 55, PANEL 2: We've seen this sort of divine revelation before in OLYMPIANS Book 3, *Hera: The Goddess and Her Glory*, when Hera reveals to Jason his true parentage.

PAGE 57, PANEL 2: As seen in OLYMPIANS Book 2, *Athena: Grey-Eyed Goddess*, and OLYMPIANS Book 3, *Hera: The Goddess and Her Glory*. In case you forgot, Alcides is the birth name of Heracles.

PAGE 65: This weird little sequence with Eros and the bee comes to us from a fragment of the lyrical poem called *The Anacreontea*. This is why I love going back to ancient sources; you come across such strange little gems.

ABOUT THIS BOOK

APHRODITE: GODDESS OF LOVE is the sixth book in *OLYMPIANS*, a graphic novel series from First Second that retells the Greek myths.

FOR DISCUSSION

1 Aphrodite is an unusual Olympian, in that she's the only one who married into the family as opposed to being related to Zeus. Why do you think that is important?

2 Paris chose Aphrodite to win the golden apple of Eris. Who would you have chosen, and why?

3 Pygmalion wished for Aphrodite to bring his statute to life. What would you wish for from Aphrodite?

4 There are several different candidates for the father of Aphrodite's son Eros put forth in this book. Who do you think was Eros's dad and why?

5 Why do you think that Zeus was so afraid of Aphrodite's power? And why do you think he wanted Paris to be the one who judged among the goddesses?

6 Eris is just about the worst person you could ever invite to a party. Why did Zeus let her into the wedding? Who else do you think would be an awful guest?

7 Very few people believe in the Greek gods today. Why do you think it is important that we still learn about them?

CHARITES

ATTENDANTS OF APHRODITE

GODDESSES OF Grace, Beauty, Adornment

ROMAN NAME The Gratiae

INDIVIDUAL NAMES Aglaia ("Glory"), Euphrosyne ("Merriment"), Thalia ("Festivity")

HEAVENLY BODIES The asteroid Charis is named after the Charites; each of the individual Charites also has an asteroid named after her.

SACRED PLACES Boeotia, the oldest site of their worship in ancient Greece

MODERN LEGACY Such modern words as charity, charisma, and grace are derived from the names of the Charites.

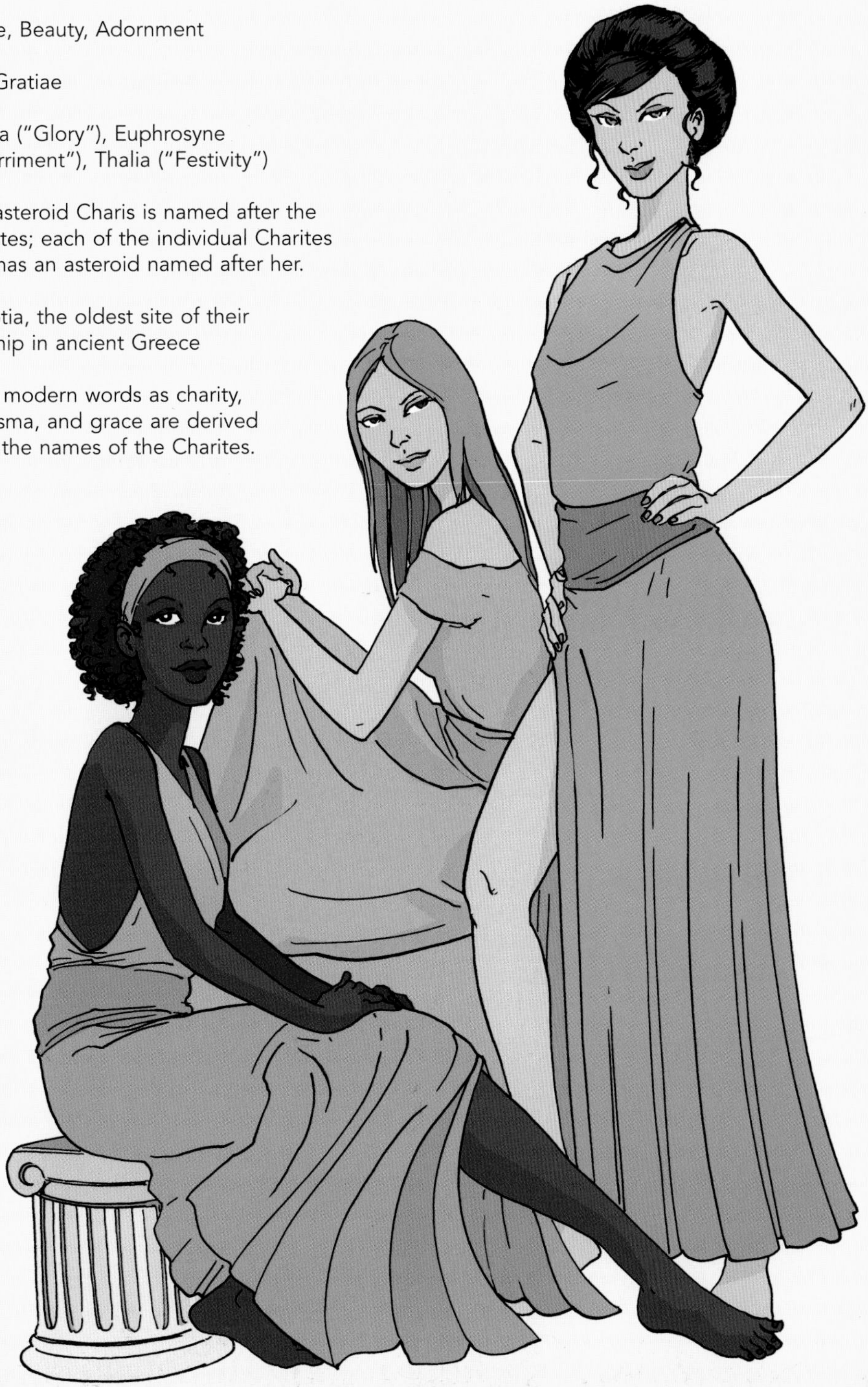

BIBLIOGRAPHY

HESIOD: VOLUME 1, THEOGENY. WORKS AND DAYS: TESTIMONIA.
NEW YORK: LOEB CLASSICAL LIBRARY, 2007.
The birth of Aphrodite from sea foam is told in many ancient sources, but Hesiod's is the version that they all draw upon.

OPPIAN, COLLUTHUS, TRYPHIODORUS. NEW YORK: LOEB CLASSICAL LIBRARY, 1928.
This book is a collection of the surviving works of the three authors after whom it is named. My retelling of the Judgment of Paris owes a lot to the version that Colluthus recounts here.

OVID. METAMORPHOSES NEW YORK: PENGUIN CLASSICS, 2004.
Actually a Roman text, so the gods all sport their Roman names, but this is the source I used for the story of Pygmalion.

THEOI GREEK MYTHOLOGY WEB SITE WWW.THEOI.COM
Without a doubt, the single most valuable resource I came across in this entire venture. At theoi.com, you can find an encyclopedia of various gods and goddesses from Greek mythology, cross referenced with every mention of them they could find in literally hundreds of ancient Greek and Roman texts. Unfortunately, it's not quite complete, and it doesn't seem to be updated anymore.

MYTH INDEX WEB SITE WWW.MYTHINDEX.COM
Another mythology Web site connected to Theoi.com. While it doesn't have the painstakingly compiled quotations from ancient texts, it does offer some impressive encyclopedic entries on virtually every character to ever pass through a Greek myth. Pretty amazing.

ALSO RECOMMENDED
FOR YOUNGER READERS

D'Aulaires' Book of Greek Myths. Ingri and Edgar Parin D'Aulaire. New York: Doubleday, 1962

We Goddesses: Athena, Aphrodite, Hera. Doris Orgel, illustrated by Marilee Heyer. New York: DK Publishing, 1999

FOR OLDER READERS

The Marriage of Cadmus and Harmony. Robert Calasso. New York: Knopf, 1993

Mythology. Edith Hamilton. New York: Grand Central Publishing, 1999

EROS
MISCHIEVOUS GODLING OF LOVE

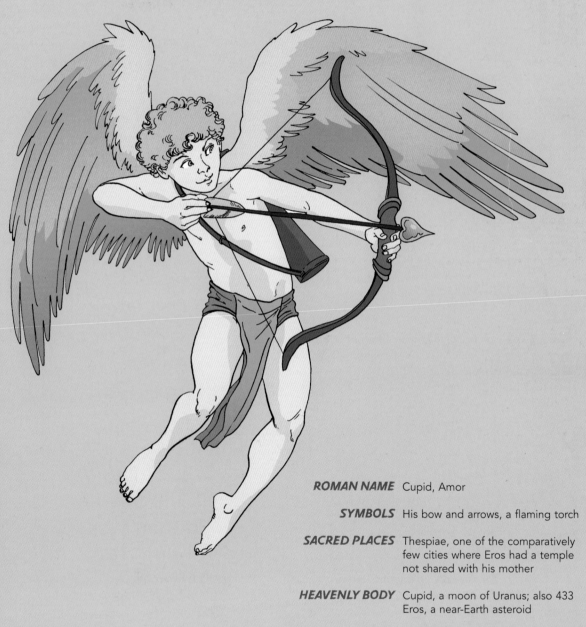

ROMAN NAME Cupid, Amor

SYMBOLS His bow and arrows, a flaming torch

SACRED PLACES Thespiae, one of the comparatively few cities where Eros had a temple not shared with his mother

HEAVENLY BODY Cupid, a moon of Uranus; also 433 Eros, a near-Earth asteroid

MODERN LEGACY Eros is still a familiar sight every February fourteenth, on Valentine's Day. As Cupid, he is one of that holiday's most prominent symbols.

To the Goddess of Love herself—thank you for letting me find Arta.

—G.O.

First Second

New York

Copyright © 2014 by George O'Connor

Published by First Second
First Second is an imprint of Roaring Brook Press,
a division of Holtzbrinck Publishing Holdings Limited Partnership
175 Fifth Avenue, New York, New York 10010

Cataloging-in-Publication Data is on file at the Library of Congress

Paperback ISBN: 978-1-59643-739-5
Hardcover ISBN: 978-1-59643-947-4

First Second books may be purchased for business or promotional use.
For information on bulk purchases please contact Macmillan Corporate
and Premium Sales Department at (800) 221-7945 x5442 or by email at
specialmarkets@macmillan.com.

First Edition 2014

Cover design by Colleen AF Venable
Book design by Rob Steen

Printed in China by Toppan Leefung Printing Ltd., Dongguan City, Guangdong Province

Hardcover 10 9 8 7 6 5 4
Paperback 10 9 8 7